Pressing Toward the Mark

a novel by
Karen Forster

*Jon and Jane,
Keep pressing toward the
Mark for God's glory!
Karen Forster
4.3.23*

Pressing Toward the Mark

Copyright © 2023 by Karen Forster

All rights reserved. No part of this publication may be reproduced, stored in a retrieval system, or transmitted by any means – electronic, mechanical, photographic (photocopying), recording, or otherwise – without prior permission in writing from the author.

This is a work of fiction. While, as in all fiction, the literary perceptions and insights are based on experience, all names, characters, places, and incidents are either products of the author's imagination or are used fictitiously. No reference to any real persons is intended or should be inferred.

All Scripture references are taken from the King James Version of the Bible.

Cover design by Laura M. Fuchs

ISBN: 979-8-218-95053-8

Printed in the United States of America

Learn more information at:
www.booksbykarenforster.blogspot.com

Preface

I am so excited to share this book with you. It has been so long in the making! <u>Pressing Toward the Mark</u> is a sequel to my book <u>Journey of Grace</u> and is filled with relatable real-life lessons woven into a riveting fictional setting. It's my prayer that as you read, you will not only be entertained, but challenged and encouraged in your walk with the God.

Do you find yourself slipping into a more tepid spiritual walk . . . one that isn't such a burning contrast to the world around you?

Do you ever struggle with being bold for Christ?

Have you found yourself at a decision point where putting Christ above all else will cost you something very dear?

These are common struggles for us as Christians, yet God, by His Word and Holy Spirit, has given us all the wisdom and strength to be gloriously victorious in every situation.

As the famous poem by C.T. Studd reminds us, "Only one life, 'twill soon be past, only what's done for Christ will last."

Friend, I am cheering you on as you "press toward the mark, for the prize of the high calling of God in Christ Jesus" (Phil. 3:14).

In, for, and because of Christ,

Karen Forster

Acknowledgments

First of all I want to thank God, from whom all blessings flow. (James 1:17) I recognize that every breath I take, and every heartbeat is a gift from Him. What is even greater is what He has done for me spiritually, giving me eternal life, and walking through life with me as my Heavenly Father and Best Friend. He is the true focus of this book.

I want to say a big thank you to all of the friends, relatives and acquaintances who have supported me in this project:

My parents and siblings, who have been so instrumental in my life, a constant voice of reason, and a wonderful team with whom I can learn and minister.

Tiffany Geer, for her insights as a former Emergency Room nurse.

Pilots, Jakob and Serena Brouillette, Jessica Richardson and Jaimie Tanabe who shared such helpful information and experience about aviation. I couldn't have written certain parts of this book without you!

My wonderful editors, Mary Mount, and my family, who spent many hours scrutinizing my writing so that you can read it without stumbling across typos and other errors!

Special thanks to Laura M. Fuchs for designing such a fantastic book cover. Thanks also to Elisha J. Fuchs and Genevieve R. Kapsner for their input.

Chapter One

Mark's whistling stopped abruptly. His phone was ringing. For some reason there was a feeling of uneasiness in his chest. For a moment, he stood without moving a muscle. Then quickly grabbing the phone out of his pocket, he cleared his throat and pushed the answer button.

"Hello, this is Mark."

"Hi. This is Mary calling from Newport Central Hospital," a woman's voice said. "We found your name and number in the wallet of Jerome Kennedy. He had you listed as an emergency contact." The woman paused waiting for a confirmation from Mark.

"Oh?" Mark had no idea about that. "Jerome's a good friend of mine. Has something happened to him?"

Pressing Toward the Mark

"He took a bad fall when rock climbing and is suffering from a severe head injury. We have been unable to get in contact with his family. He's in very critical condition right now. Would you be able to come to the hospital?"

There was a slight pause before Mark could answer. "Yes. I'll come right away," he said in a low, shaky voice. "Is he conscious?"

"No, he is not."

"Alright. Thank you for calling me. I'll be there as soon as I can."

Mark stood in shock for a minute, a million thoughts flying through his mind. Would Jerome live? Would he ever be the same again? And what about his salvation? Did Jerome even know the Lord? Suddenly a burning tingle surged through Mark's body. He knew he had failed to ever share the gospel with Jerome. Now the question stared him in the face: "Why, Mark? Why haven't you told him? Why have you shared about so many things with him, but never about Christ's sacrifice for him?"

God, please give me one more chance to witness to Jerome. I know I should have done it long ago. Please, don't let him die without hearing and receiving the gospel! I ask, Lord, that you would wake him up, at least long enough for me to tell him. I'm sorry for failing You ... again.

Mark's mind continued to whirl as he drove the eight miles to the hospital. Although outwardly he seemed calm and peaceful, inside his heart was crushed.

Pressing Toward the Mark

"We are doing everything we can to prevent increased ICP (intracranial pressure)," the short, wide-eyed doctor explained. "If we succeed in this, he may have a chance of living. We may need to do surgery to remove the excess blood pooling around his brain if the bleeding can't be controlled otherwise. Honestly, things do not look very promising. The head injury is by far the most serious issue, but he also broke three ribs, his collarbone, and one of his lungs is punctured."

Mark's eyes turned downward to the green tile floor. "Doctor," he said, still staring at the floor, "Is there any chance of him waking up any time soon? I really need to talk to him, just for a few minutes."

"Not really. In order to control the pressure on his brain, we've put him on some pretty strong medications which deepen his unconsciousness and put him in a paralyzed state temporarily."

"Oh . . . ." Mark nodded slowly as the realization hit him. *I might not have the chance.*

The doctor interrupted his thoughts. "Do you have a way to contact Jerome's family? As his emergency contact, that's one important thing you can help us with."

"No," Mark responded trying to think. "I don't know any of his family, and unfortunately I don't have their contact information either."

Pressing Toward the Mark

"Hmm. At least he has you here for the time being. Would you like to go in and see him briefly? As I said, he's completely unconscious and not a pretty sight in his condition."

Mark nodded.

The room where Jerome lay was dimly lit. A lump formed in Mark's throat as his eyes adjusted and he took in the painful scene before him. The once-lively Jerome rested completely still, his head slightly elevated. His chest moved steadily up and down as the ventilator did his breathing for him. Mark's stomach began to hurt as he viewed the countless wires and tubes hooked up to his friend. He let out a labored sigh and returned to the waiting room.

Two hours went by and the doctor informed Mark that they were taking Jerome into surgery to relieve pressure on his brain. As Mark waited and prayed, the time seemed to drag on forever. His mind wandered back over the events of the past three months . . . and back to that one painful day in May.

Mark combed his dark wavy hair a second time and adjusted his dress shirt collar. For multiple reasons, he wanted to look his best today. It was his sister Grace's wedding day and much more than that.

Grace and Zack had begun courting the previous summer. Shortly after their engagement, Mark had started a courtship with Hannah Kallenbach, a sweet young lady who loved her

Savior Jesus. Hannah was also one of Grace's closest friends. The Kallenbachs accepted Grace and Mark as part of the family, and the thought of Mark marrying their eldest daughter seemed natural to all.

Though Grace and Zack had planned for a short engagement, the wedding had been postponed several months due to a medical emergency in the Kallenbach family. Their 19-year-old son, Seth, who had Down Syndrome, required two major heart surgeries at the beginning of the year. These unexpected challenges drew the family and their friends closer together, and the delayed wedding day only seemed more golden. Even though the Kallenbachs were not immediate family of the bride and groom, they were highly involved in the wedding. Mr. Kallenbach had worked diligently preparing to officiate the wedding. His wife kept all of the wedding details in her mind and helped tremendously in bringing everything together. Hannah was to be the maid of honor - the most lovely one that ever was, Mark thought. What joy he would have as the best man, to walk this virtuous woman down the aisle. Finally, the day had arrived. The sky was overcast, and drizzles of rain came down at indeterminable intervals. The gloominess of the weather seemed easily overpowered by the joy and excitement of the special day.

Mark entered the church foyer. The wedding wouldn't be starting for another two hours. The families and wedding party had decided to get there early so as to leave plenty of extra time. Excitement surged through Mark's body. He had some important things to do today. And there was one particular thing he was planning, that no one else knew about. First he planned to pull Mr. Kallenbach aside and ask him for permission to marry his daughter. Then, later in the day after the wedding, he would propose to Hannah. It would be a special day to be remembered for the rest of his life.

Mark was a gentle yet strong and confident young man with a great sense of humor. He was known to think before speaking, while at the same time, maintaining an ambitious and spontaneous spirit about life. People naturally enjoyed his companionship and enthusiasm. He had big visions and a plan of how to make them become reality.

Everything in the church was relatively quiet. Mark ran through once more in his mind what he was going to say. Then, with determination, he headed downstairs to the dining hall to look for Mr. Kallenbach. His fingers were cold, yet his face felt like it was on fire. Mr. Kallenbach was sitting at a table going over his notes for the ceremony. He looked up and smiled when Mark approached him.

"Where is everyone else?" Mark asked.

"I believe the ladies are doing their hair. Some of the guys are getting things set up in the foyer, and I'm really not sure where everybody else went. I decided go over the order of events again, so I get it right when the time comes. What are you up to?"

Mark sat down in the chair across the table, facing Mr. Kallenbach. "Well, I have something I wanted to talk to you about. Do you have a few minutes?"

"Sure, Mark." Mr. Kallenbach, sensing Mark's seriousness closed his folder and gave him his full attention.

"Mr. Kallenbach, I wanted to ask you…about Hannah. I mean, I'm asking for your permission to marry her." Without stopping, or reading the look on Mr. Kallenbach's face, Mark continued. "I love her so very much and through these months of our courtship, I've seen what a special young woman she is, and I believe she's the woman God has for me. Would you give us your blessing to be married?" Mark took a deep breath and waited for the response. But before Mr. Kallenbach said a word, Mark realized something was wrong. Hannah's father leaned forward with a pained look in his eyes.

"Mark...I'm not sure what to say. I've needed to have a conversation with you about this, but I was planning to wait until after the wedding. I wish this hadn't come up today . . . ." He looked down at his folder on the table. Mark could see that under Mr. Kallenbach's big beard his face was becoming very red.

Mark's cold fingers were now tingling, and he sat still in dreadful anticipation of what Mr. Kallenbach might say next.

"You know that you're like a son to me, and that all my family absolutely loves you. I don't want that to change. And it pains me to have to tell you this, Mark, but, we are going to have to break off the courtship for now. Hannah, my wife, and I have been praying a lot about this over the past few weeks. As you know, Mark, Hannah has a heart for sharing the gospel, and she feels called to be a missionary. These past months of your courtship, we've been grieved that you don't seem to have that same vision. As I said, this has been on our minds a lot. You don't seem to be as excited about witnessing to the lost as you used to be. Hannah noticed this before her mom and I talked to her about it, and she said it has really troubled her. The three of us decided last week that the courtship should not be continued. But Mark, you should know that this is as hard for Hannah as it is for you. She loves you. She just doesn't see a way it can work."

Mark sat staring in front of him, breathless as if someone had pressed all the air out of him. His eyes were dry and burning, his mind was running in a million directions, and his heart felt more sick than he ever knew it could.

"I'm so sorry I had to tell you this today, of all days," Mr. Kallenbach said after a moment of silence. He reached across the table and put a hand on Mark's shoulder. "Son, please know that we still love you, and we still want to be here for you. I know today is going to be a hard day for you... especially with you being the best man and Hannah the maid of honor. I wish I could make this easier for you. I won't tell Hannah that we've talked until tomorrow, if you'd prefer."

Mark nodded half absentmindedly. How he wished he could wake up and find that this was all a bad dream! No words seemed right. What could he say? Everything would be different now.

Chapter Two

After Mark's conversation with Mr. Kallenbach, he immediately sought a quiet place where he could be alone to think. He found a suitable place in a small deserted classroom down the long church hallway. He slumped down on the floor against the wall and put his hands over his face. For a few minutes his mind almost froze. The pain and shock was overwhelming his ability to think. At the same time so many feelings began to well up inside his body. Disappointment, hurt, fear, anger. *What now? What now?* he asked himself almost in a panic. He needed much more than a few minutes to think about it all, but yet in just 90 minutes the wedding ceremony would be starting. *And Hannah . . . I have to walk her down the aisle. How will I ever make it through this day? But this is Grace's day. I can't let her sense that something is wrong.*

Mark straightened his tie and looked himself over in the mirror one more time. *I think I look pretty normal.* He took a deep breath and opened the door, entering the foyer again. His mother noticed him as she hurriedly made her way around.

"There you are, Son. I've been asking for you, but no one knew where you were." She quickly glanced up at his handsome face. "Are you alright?"

"Um, Mom, what am I supposed to be doing right now?" Mark asked, avoiding the question.

"Oh, I'm not exactly sure. Go ask Lisa Kallenbach. She's doing the coordinating for the bridal party. Oh look, some guests are here already!" She quickly patted his arm and gave him a mother's 'I-love-you-and-you-look-amazing' look and hurried on with her work. Mark meandered over to the back room where the groomsmen were sitting around chatting. Zack sat among them looking as sharp, content and happy as ever. Mark didn't think he had ever seen a groom so well-tempered and relaxed before his wedding. For a brief moment he imagined himself in Zack's place, and then the pain struck him that the girl he loved wouldn't marry him. He felt a surge of sadness and self-pity overtaking him. *No!* he told himself, *I can't let this control me. I have to act normal for the wedding.*

The church quickly filled with guests, and the ushers directed everyone to seats. Mrs. Kallenbach had not checked in on the groomsmen since Mark had joined them. She found herself more needed with the girls, who were still getting themselves ready. Grace, though it was her wedding day, remained calm and thoughtful. However, at times others were a little frustrated with her because her thoughts were so filled with one person, and she didn't think about much else unless someone drew her attention to it.

The wedding began with a few congregational hymns. Grace and Zack both wanted the wedding to be focused on the Lord and thought praising God in song would be a good way to start. Zack stood at the podium directing the music. The rest of the bridal party assembled in the church foyer. Mrs. Kallenbach helped each pair get in place.

Mark stood in the place where he was told. He tried not to let himself drift into his own world of despair. Naturally, he stared at the floor, but then he would catch himself and jerk his head up trying to look bright-eyed and cheery. He glanced over at Hannah. She looked as beautiful as ever with her sweet face and long, dark hair. She looked happy.

Mrs. Kallenbach tapped Mark on the shoulder. "Mark, are you ready?" Something in her voice was like a mother's loving care for a wound that needed to be bandaged. Her husband had briefly told her about the conversation he had with Mark. She felt deeply sorry for Mark, knowing that he was probably feeling the most pain he had likely ever known.

The processional began, and Mrs. Kallenbach gave each pair of bridesmaids and groomsmen their signal when they were to start down the aisle. When it was their turn, Mark held out his arm to escort Hannah down the aisle. As she linked her arm in his, a stark tingle ran through his body. He wondered if Hannah could feel it too. No, she didn't care for him like she used to ... or maybe she never did really love him. If circumstances had been different, he would have enjoyed that gentle touch, but now he had to ignore the painful distraction and proceed with a smile. Hannah walked gracefully by his side smiling with true happiness for her close friend Grace. She looked over the congregation and spotted the place near the front where her dear family was seated – all eight of her brothers, her baby sister, and her oldest brother's wife. A large family is one thing she and Mark did not have in common. He only had his younger sister, Grace, who was getting married today.

The wedding ceremony seemed short yet eternally long to Mark. With a feverish headache, he witnessed as his sister and her groom exchanged their personalized vows, their rings, and their first kiss. What a sweet thing it was to watch! Yet the pain in his own heart created within him a numb burning that wouldn't subside.

That night Mark arrived home exhausted. The first thing he noticed when he entered the house was that Grace was not there to greet him. For the past year she had lived with him and he had grown accustomed to his sister preparing their meals, washing all the laundry, and keeping the house. But now she would have her own home and a husband to take care of.

Loosening his tie and unbuttoning the top buttons of his shirt, he sat down at the desk in his room. His head sunk into his hot sweaty hands, and he sat there for quite a few minutes without moving again. His mind drifted back to Hannah. *What am I to do now?* Something needed to change. He needed to take a step in a new direction. *I need to get out of this place . . . go somewhere far away for a while . . . get a fresh start . . . see new things . . . meet new people.*

The following Monday, Mark informed his employer that he was going to be leaving. The man was very disappointed. He knew that finding another man as hard working and skilled in plumbing as Mark would be difficult. Nonetheless, Mark's mind was made up.

It was Friday morning, six days since Grace and Zack's wedding. Six days since his courtship with Hannah had been broken. Mark looked over his bags in the trunk one last time before shutting it. Everything was ready to go. With determination, he got into his forest green Toyota Camry, and headed out of town.

Chapter Three

*J*essa glanced in her rear view mirror for two reasons: one, to make sure no one was following, and two, to see the city's "welcome" sign getting smaller.

"They've gone too far this time." She pressed on the gas pedal matching the anger in her heart. Her parents just didn't understand, she thought. They hadn't even met Jerome in person, and yet they already discredited him. She wanted to marry for more than money and politics. She hoped what she would uncover in Georgia would finally prove to her father that her boyfriend, Jerome, was *not* a loser.

Her email to Jerome earlier that morning had been short and serious. *My dad forbids me from seeing you any more. I don't know what to say.... I'm mad and I'm going to Georgia. Don't follow me... for your own sake.*

Pressing Toward the Mark

Jessa was a small, agile young woman who always had a mysterious, spirited sparkle in her eye. Rules, to her, were boundaries begging to be pushed or broken. Unknowns in the future were irresistible challenges beckoning her to surmount them. She was not willing to live life being tied to a career she couldn't easily get away from or juggling the nuisance and responsibility of finances, loans, and loads of money. And politics... that had to be one of the worst irritations to her. "Stop trying to please and manipulate people and just be the way you want to be," she would argue.

Now was her chance to get away from all that bothered her and breathe some fresh air... experience some fresh surroundings for awhile. She'd handle the consequences later. She was sure the answers to her restless thoughts would be found in Georgia. Her sweet grandmother lived in the southern part of the state on the edge of a 12-acre orange grove. Many sweet memories were made in that orchard throughout Jessa's childhood. Since she and her parents had moved to California, she hadn't seen her grandma very often.

Visiting her grandmother was not the only thing on Jessa's mind. First she would travel to Griffin, Georgia – Jerome's hometown - to find out the rest of his story. He had told her that his father was a well-known geologist who had traveled the world and wanted his son to follow in his steps. Jerome had studied diligently and was doing well in college until something happened. Something about an older lady "who needed moral support" as Jerome put it. Somehow this lady impacted Jerome's ability to complete college, and he never finished.

Jessa wanted the full story. With all her heart she hoped it would reveal that the man she loved was worthy of her father's acceptance . . . and not the opposite.

The redness of Hannah's bloodshot eyes reflected back at her on the black screen of her phone. She pushed the power button on top and closed her eyes, praying for God to guide her words and heal her heart. After letting out a deep breath, she began to write a text to Mark.

Mark, I pray with all my heart you are doing okay. I wanted to tell you I'm sorry things between us ended the way they did. I hope you can understand. I respect you greatly, and I know God wants to use you powerfully. And I pray so much that you listen to Him and follow Him with everything in you. P.S My brothers wanted me to make sure you'll be here for church on Sunday.

"There," she said hitting send. "If he only knew how much I still love him." She wished so much that things would change. She prayed that they still would. If only Mark would find that zeal and excitement for the Lord's work again.

Richard Keller glared at the picture of Jerome on his daughter Jessa's laptop. "I'm surprised she didn't take her computer when she left," he mumbled to himself. Determined to find out where she went, he began to look through her recent emails. "Aha! Here's one to Jerome. Let's see . . . . 'I'm mad and I'm going to Georgia. Don't follow me . . . for your own sake. ~Jessa.'" Mr. Keller looked out the window. *Oh, he'll follow her alright. They'll probably meet up in Georgia and get married before I can stop them! I know what I'll do. The guy doesn't have much backbone. I'll give him a "friendly" call and warn him to stay away from my daughter!*

"Denver - 15 miles," Mark read aloud to himself. He had spent the past two days driving the 1000 miles from Indianapolis to Denver, Colorado. Why Denver? For some reason it just seemed right to him and he decided to go. And now, here he was, just fifteen miles from his destination. What would await him there? Anything? He pulled in at a small hotel. The sign out front read, *Dine*ver Hotel & Diner. "Hopefully this place will be decent enough," Mark said under his breath as he got out of his car.

Inside there was a little front desk, but no one was present. There was a piece of paper on the desk that read, "I'll be gone for just about an hour. Will be back around 5:30. Thank you!" Mark turned around to leave, but just as he did so, a woman came around the corner from the hall.

"Oh, would you like me to call her and let her know you're here? You want to get a room, right?"

"Yes."

"Well I have her number, so I can give her a call. Just hold on."

"Okay, thanks."

The woman took out her cell phone and began to dial the number on the business card in her hand. As she did so, a minivan drove up outside. A few moments later a woman walked in the front doors, apologizing for not being there when he had arrived. She was carrying a chubby, smiley baby boy on her hip. Four other children meandered in after her. *Cute kids,* Mark thought. He had always loved children, and these were especially cute ones with their coal black hair and Native American features.

"Now, what can I do for you?" the lady said, stepping behind the front desk smiling. She was a blonde-haired woman with a fair completion; a stark contrast to her children. She cleared off some papers from the desk and moved the computer mouse to wake up the screen.

"Um, I'd like to get a room. I might be in the area for a while . . . so, do you have anything available for an extended stay?" He wasn't sure yet of his plans for the next few weeks.

"Certainly. Let me see here . . . ." She typed a few words with her one free hand and looked at the options. The toddler she held seemed to be a friendly little tyke, who did his best to engage in a playful, wordless conversation with Mark. "Okay." She looked up from the computer. "The Forest Room on third floor is available. Do you think you'll be here for a couple weeks?"

"Probably, but I don't know for sure yet."

Pressing Toward the Mark

"That's just fine. I'll put you down for a two-week stay and if you need to cancel, just let me know a few days before you'll be leaving."

"That would be great. Thanks," Mark said appreciatively.

"I'm Shawna Wanbli," the woman said, introducing herself. "My husband and I own the hotel. Our family lives here on site and we do our best to serve our guests and make their time here comfortable. I hope you enjoy your stay with us!"

"Thank you! I think it's neat that you run this place as a family."

Shawna nodded with a smile and proceeded to finish Mark's hotel reservation with further information from him. She turned from the computer for a moment and called for one of her children. "Adella, please go make sure there are towel sets in the Forest Room." The nine-year-old sprinted away down the hall to complete the errand.

Minutes later, as Mark made his way down the hall, he passed a room which had its door half-way open. He could tell by the way it looked that this was the room in which the owners' family lived. Right outside the door, in the hall, there was a congregation of kids' shoes and flip-flops. A smile crept across his face. This really was a family-operated hotel. He wondered how much he would interact with the family during the next two weeks or so.

Hello Tamaya! Hannah began her letter. She was interested to see where this endeavor would go. This fifteen-year-old girl lived across the world in Botswana, Africa. A missionary family who lived in Tamaya's village had asked Hannah to help mentor the girl through letters. She was happy to take the opportunity and be used of the Lord in Tamaya's life. *Since this is the first letter, I should probably tell her a little about my family.* Hannah stared at the paper in front of her and twiddled with the pen between her fingers. After a moment of thought, she resumed writing.

My name is Hannah, and I'm excited to get to know you! Let me tell you about me and my family.

My dad and mom are Ben and Lisa. Dad works hard here on our farm, managing our greenhouse and aquaponics business. (Aquaponics is a fancy word that means we grow fish in tanks inside the greenhouse, and they help fertilize the water we use for the plants.) Mom home schools my younger siblings and is very diligent in making meals, cleaning the house, and taking care of everyone.

I have an older brother named Charlie. He is married to Sarah, and they have a baby girl, "Annie." Her real name is Hannah, like me, but we call her Annie so it isn't confusing.

I am the second oldest, and I am 21. I like to go for walks and enjoy the outdoors. I value spending time with people I love. The Bible is my favorite book in the whole world, and it effects my whole life. (I hope you and I can talk more and learn from the Bible together through our letters!)

After me, there is Seth, who is 19. He has Down Syndrome. He can't do a lot of things others his age can, but one thing he does better than the rest of us is SMILE... A LOT! :-) I'm thankful for every one of my siblings. Each one is a special, unique gift.

Joey is next. He is 17, and he makes us laugh a lot! He has a very positive outlook on every situation and loves to come up with big ideas and plans.

Daniel is 14. He is a lot quieter than Joey. He has a kind heart. He is becoming our family mechanic. He loves to fix cars and farm machinery. What a blessing that has been for us!

Then there is Tyler, who is nine. He likes to watch and help Daniel with his mechanic work. He is very detail oriented and usually keeps his things neat and organized.

Willie is six. He is a bit like Joey in his personality... always looking for adventure, loving to experiment... even if it means making an accidental explosion like he and Joey did yesterday during their "science experiment." :-)

Then I have twin brothers, Jedidiah and Phillip. They are five years old. They love to play with each other. It's so cute. They're best friends!

Heather Rose is the youngest. She's three, and so very cute! She's talking a lot now and loves to "help" with chores on the farm.

So that's my family! Please tell me all about you and your family! Do you have brothers or sisters? What do you like to do for fun? What is your favorite Bible verse? My favorite passage is Psalm 73:25-26. "Whom have I in heaven but thee? *and there is* none *upon earth that* I *desire beside thee.* My flesh and my heart faileth: *but* God *is* the strength of my heart, and my portion for ever."

I hope you have a wonderful day, and I look forward to hearing from you!

Your new friend,

Hannah

Mark sat down on the bench outside of McDonalds and took his laptop out of its bag. *It's a nice day to be outside. I might as well not sit inside if I can get internet connection out here.*

"No connections available," the computer notification popped up.

"Ugh!" Mark sighed closing his laptop. "So much for doing my work outside. Why can't it connect from out here?"

"All you need to do is sit right up next to the building. Like over there on the grass. That's where I like to do it," a sandy-haired young man said, gesturing with one hand, his other hand on his hip. "But make sure your back is resting against the building, 'cause if you stop leaning on the building the Wi-Fi won't work."

Mark squinted up at the young fellow, not sure whether to restrain the chuckle that was about to come or not. He wore a bright tie-dyed bandana around his forehead like a sweat band. It seemed to fit his character pretty well.

"Well, just kidding, about the last part," the young man continued light-heartedly. "The Wi-Fi does work better over there, but you don't have to lean on the building."

"Okay, thanks."

"I'm Jerome, by the way. I'm sure I'll see you again if you plan on sticking around at all. I've been coming here for lunch every day lately. Don't ask me how I got into the habit; I know it's terrible!"

"Good to meet you, Jerome. I'm Mark."

"Well, Mark, enjoy the nice day!" Jerome turned and dashed away across the parking lot.

The next day Mark ran into Jerome again at McDonald's. Although Mark didn't usually eat fast food, the hotel only provided breakfast with his room rate. Lunch and supper were provided for an additional cost, but he thought McDonald's would be cheaper. Besides this, he felt like getting out for a while. He wasn't used to having no one to talk to. When his new acquaintance, the self-appointed McDonald's greeter, suggested that they have their lunch together, Mark gladly agreed.

This was the beginning of a strong friendship that would develop between them over the coming weeks and months.

Jerome was a spirited, energetic, adventurous fellow with a wild imagination. He did not like to stay in one place long. His pattern was to arrive at somewhere new and unknown, explore, get the thrill of whatever adventure there might be, see what there is to see, give people something interesting to talk about, and move on.

Mark found himself absorbed in Jerome's stories. He had been so many places and done so many things! Jerome loved to talk, and Mark loved to listen.

"So how did you end up here?" Mark asked after hearing about one of Jerome's rock climbing experiences.

"I was hitch-hiking my way across the country from California, hoping to eventually land in Georgia. A bushy bearded, lumberjack-type fella picked me up and brought me this far. From here he was heading north, so I decided to explore the Denver area for a few days. And then . . . some other things happened that complicated my plans."

"So how long have you been here?"

"Ah, let's see, I think it's been about a week. I kinda like this state, and things keep grabbing my attention and begging me to investigate them. Say, are you into rock climbing at all?"

"Well . . . I've actually never tried it."

"Do you want to? I'll show you how! I only have gear for myself, but I know of a place you can rent gear from. I think their prices are pretty reasonable."

"Let me think about it and get back to you. Will you be here tomorrow?"

"You can count on it!"

Pressing Toward the Mark

Hannah set her Bible down on the bed another time and stared down at it. She gently laid her hand over it and moved her lips in an almost silent prayer. *Lord, why is it that I only feel peace when I'm reading this Book? Thank You so much for giving me Your Word.* She let out a thankful sigh and picked up her Bible again. *Thank You for never changing and for always being faithful, Lord.* Since her friend Grace's wedding, Hannah had not seemed herself. No one in her family had to guess why. Her heart was torn. Her love for Jesus had taken first priority in her decisions, and this meant breaking off the courtship with the man she loved sincerely. She knew she had made the right choice, but that didn't take away from the pain she felt. Now that the wedding was over, Grace, who had been her best friend, was on a delightful honeymoon. She had probably forgotten all about Hannah, and everyone back home. And Mark? What had become of him? He had replied to her text in few words . . . words that seemed cold, hardened, and unwilling to let anyone near. He was out of town and wouldn't be coming for church on Sunday. No one had heard any other details. Hannah wanted to know more about it, but every time she thought of inquiring, something inside held her back.

Never before had she felt such a longing for the Word of God and to have a closer walk with her Savior. At times throughout the day an overwhelming load of thoughts and emotions would wash over her, and she would slip away to the quiet of her room. There she would get on her knees and pour out her heart to the Lord. Oh the peace that came when she cast her cares upon Him! And His Word - it never ceased to speak to her heart and strengthen her spirit. It was in those quiet moments alone with God that her deepest needs were met. He alone could satisfy her.

Chapter Four

The sun was scorching hot as the two young men walked down the path back to the parking lot carrying their rock climbing gear. Mark wiped the perspiration from his forehead. Jerome was not nearly as hot and exhausted as his companion. However, though he wouldn't want to admit it, his tie-dyed bandana around his forehead was nearly soaked with sweat.

"I can tell you're used to this," Mark said, when they reached the car and took a break for water.

"Well, yeah, I am. And what did you think of scaling? Wanna do it again?"

"Yeah, I guess I do!"

"You know, you're what we'd call a 'Gumby' in rock climbing lingo."

Pressing Toward the Mark

"What does it mean?"

"It means you're new at it and don't know what you're doing," Jerome said matter-of-factly. "But you're a smart Gumby, and you'll catch on fast. You don't know how glad I am to have someone to scale with me! When I was a teenager, I had three buddies that would go out climbing with me all the time. Then as we got older, we parted ways, and for a while I was on my own. Then I met Jessa." He paused for a moment and stared thoughtfully at his water bottle. "She loved rock climbing, and we had so many great times together. That was our kind of date: hike out along the bottom of the cliff, find the perfect spot, and then start climbing. She always insisted that we bring lunch along too, and we'd have a little picnic before heading back." There was a small crack in Jerome's voice, and he uncomfortably glanced from side to side and then at the ground.

"So what happened? I mean, where'd she go?"

"I'm not sure . . . . Somewhere in Georgia I guess. A couple weeks ago she sent me an email telling me she was leaving town and that I was not to follow her."

"Do you have any idea why she left?"

"It's her father. She always told me how he was a strict, religious man who wanted her to marry into a wealthy and socially popular family. *I* don't fit his criteria, and he wasn't happy about us dating. In fact, I've never even seen the man because he doesn't want to meet me. At first I didn't understand why Jessa said not to follow her, and I started hitch-hiking my way to Georgia . . . only got this far, as you know. A few days later I got a phone call from her dad threatening me and saying I better leave his daughter alone. It was then that I realized this was all happening because of him, and Jessa had warned me not to follow her for my own sake because of her father. I keep getting texts, calls, and emails from her dad calling me all sorts of names and saying it's my fault she left. A few days ago he sent a text saying, 'You have no right to run off with my daughter, and if you don't bring her back immediately I'm going to get the police involved!' It suddenly dawned on me that he thought Jessa and I had run off *together*! I told him I didn't know where she was, but he said I was a liar. So right now, I don't really know what I'm doing. I don't dare go to Georgia like I was planning to."

Mark was silent for a moment and then said, "You sure do live an interesting life, don't you, Jerome." A tinge of sadness surged through him, knowing what it was like to have the one you love slip out of reach.

"She hasn't replied to my calls or texts recently so I don't know what to think. Maybe she really doesn't want to see me."

The two stood quietly thinking and then Jerome broke the silence. "Well, Gumby, let's finish loading up and get you back to the hotel."

"Mark, everyone has been worried about you!" Even over the phone he could hear the slight hint of frustration in Grace's voice. "Why didn't you tell anyone you were leaving?"

"I'm having a hard time with it all, Grace. Just give me some time."

"I know...." her voice softened and trailed off as she thought about the heartbreak her older brother must be feeling. "Have you called the Kallenbachs since the wedding?" She almost didn't want to mention Hannah's name.

"No."

"I really am sorry about how it all happened, Mark. I wish things could have been different . . . and maybe someday they will be . . . ."

What was she saying? That someday things between him and Hannah would work out? Not a chance . . . or at least not a very big one. He brushed the thought away. "I just had to get away from things and go somewhere to think and get a fresh start. I'll be okay."

"How long will you be gone?"

"I don't know yet. I'm having a good time here actually. The mountains are beautiful, and I'm actually learning some rock climbing basics!"

"Mark! You can't go rock climbing alone! That's way too dangerous! You'll get yourself killed. I'm about ready to come out there and get you myself. You might be thinking but you're not thinking straight!"

"Whoa, whoa, whoa, Little Sister," he said smirking. "I didn't say I went alone."

"Well, who went with you?"

"You mean, who did I go with?"

"Okay, sure."

"I met a guy the first day here that loves the sport and is teaching me the ropes . . . literally." Mark chuckled at his pun. "He's actually a really fun guy."

Grace was glad to hear Mark sounding more like himself again – always with a joke or pun – and looking on the bright side of things. "Well, be safe, and keep me updated on your progress."

"I'll try."

"I wish there was something I could do to help you."

"With rock climbing?"

"No," she rolled her eyes smiling. "I wish I could take some of your hurt for you, or do something to heal your heart . . . and Hannah's too."

He felt momentarily like his heart would be okay, until she said that name. "Thanks, Sis. I'll be okay."

"I'm praying for you. God does have a plan in all of this, Mark."

"Thanks. I hope so."

"Sleep well tonight."

"You too, Grace. Say 'Hi' to Zack for me."

"Will do."

Mark tossed the phone onto the bed next to him, then blew out a heavy sigh, and combed his fingers through his hair. *What now? I've been sitting around for too long. I don't have anything going on with Jerome today, and there's nothing to do. I've been here for two weeks already. I need to make some plans.* As Mark sat thinking, he felt the Holy Spirit convicting him of wasting time over the past weeks. Yes, he needed time to think, to heal, and to rest. But what was he doing with his life? Time is a gift from God. Was he "redeeming the time because the days are evil" or was he simply letting time pass by? "I need to find some work," he said out loud. With that he stood up and walked down the hall. He found, Elu Wanbli, Shawna's husband, in the lobby working at the front desk. Mark had gotten to know this kind Native American man during his stay and appreciated how God was a part of everything in his life.

"Hello, Mark. How are you, My Friend?" Elu greeted.

"I'm fine, thanks, Elu. Do you happen to know where I might find a job around here? Are there any stores or businesses that are hiring?"

"What type of work do you want?"

"Oh, I don't know . . . ."

"How about replacing light bulbs and fixing toilets, and doing electrical? You know how?"

"More or less," Mark answered with a curious look on his face.

"Then you can work for me, here at the hotel! Here, come sit down at one of the tables with me and we will talk about an agreement."

"Well, okay."

Pressing Toward the Mark

Elu shuffled some papers around behind the desk, before finding the one he was looking for. "Okay," he said sitting down across from Mark and placing a very long list on the table. Here's a list of things we need to do now. There are always more things too."

"Wow! Looks like you have enough to keep me busy for a while!"

"Yes, My Friend! If you can help, you are a gift from God! Now, let's talk about your pay."

Thank you, Lord, for leading me to this place! Mark prayed silently. *I know You're looking out for me.*

The two men discussed details and agreed that Mark would work like part of the family, earning his room and board at the hotel . . . including lunch and supper. No more need for fast food!

Richard Keller slipped his phone into his shirt pocket and jotted a note down on the pad of paper from his briefcase. "There," he said to himself. "Hope the hotel is decent . . . if it's not, I don't have any other choices unless I want to relocate every couple days."

His phone came alive again with a loud ring. Seeing it was his wife calling, he answered with a tired, "Hi Marge."

"How was the trip? Did you get to your hotel yet?"

"The trip was fine, but my hotel reservations got mixed up somehow and they had me scheduled for next month. I called all over the place trying to find another hotel that had a room available for two straight weeks. It's impossible to find last minute like this."

"What are you going to do?"

"I found one family-owned hotel that has a room available. Costs half what the other place charges. I hope it's not a garbage heap." His attitude was not the least enthusiastic.

"Hmmm. Well, I'm glad you found something...." Her voice trailed off as she held her tongue from asking him to just come back home. "Richard, I'm not sure I'm ready to be here at home two weeks with both you and Jessa being gone. Have you heard *anything* from her? She's been gone for almost six weeks!" There was more than loneliness in her voice. It was concern.

"No." His tone was harsh yet indicating that he was hurting inside.

"Do you think it was our fault that she left? I mean, did we push too hard?"

"Don't go making excuses for our foolish daughter!" he roared. "She knows better than to run off with some uneducated, wander-foot punk of a boyfriend! And what's wrong with the man we wanted her to marry, Margaret? James comes from a well-to-do family with all the money and social connections she could want. He and Jessa could make a great life together."

"If they loved each other," his wife added gently.

Pressing Toward the Mark

Silence claimed the line for a moment, and then he concluded, "If she is not back home by the time I return from this business trip, then I *am* going to get the police involved."

"I'll call you later, Richard."

Returning the phone to his pocket again he sat staring for a minute. "Why does life have to be so complicated?"

"Good afternoon," Mr. Keller said as he approached the hotel reception desk. He was wearing his usual business attire: a personally tailored suit and a tie that was so tight it looked as if he should be struggling for air.

Mrs. Wanbli looked up smiling. "What can I do for you, Sir?"

"I am Mr. Richard Keller," he said, expecting this to be enough of an explanation.

She hesitated and then her face lit up. "Oh yes, Mr. Keller! We're glad you've arrived! Are you still planning to stay for two weeks?"

"Yes, that is my intention, but we will see," he said dryly as he surveyed his surroundings.

"Very good, Mr. Keller," she said standing. "Let me show you to your room."

Pressing Toward the Mark

    It was a hot, muggy day in Griffin, Georgia. Jessa pulled a bright tie-dyed bandana out of her pocket and wiped the sweat from her brow. This bandana was a gift from Jerome that she took with her everywhere. She glanced up at the sign outside the store building again. "Yup, this is the place!" She took a deep breath and tightened her ponytail before entering the small-town thrift store. The aroma of rich roasted coffee greeted her and she looked around questioning whether this was really a second-hand store or a coffee shop under cover. Several tables with chairs claimed the bright sunny spot by the large storefront windows. A few people leisurely sipped their drinks, either chatting with a friend, reading a book, or working on their laptop. It looked so inviting! Jessa turned to see what else this special building had to offer. The many racks loaded with clothing, and shelves full of miscellaneous toys, games and gadgets lent to the fact that this really was a thrift store.

    A woman wearing a cute yet practical apron addressed her. "Welcome! Is this your first time here? I don't recall seeing you before."

    "Yes, I'm from out of town, but a friend told me about this place."

    "Wonderful! We're glad you stopped by! I hope you'll stick around for a while and grab a cup of coffee." She gestured in the direction of the big windows.

    "So, this is a thrift store . . . with a coffee shop in it?" Jessa had never heard of such a thing.

    "Yes, it's pretty special, isn't it? We decided to add the coffee shop aspect because it supports the friendly and social aspect of our store. Not only do we want people to find good deals on used items here, but we want them to make friends, and have a great day!"

"I love that idea! I wonder why Jerome never mentioned you had a coffee shop."

"Well, we've only had the coffee shop for about six months. Wait, Honey, did you say Jerome?"

"Yeah, he used to work here," Jessa explained.

"Oh, I know! I could never forget Jerome. He was such a bright spot around here….I knew him since he was a little boy. I've wondered what ever happened to him. Haven't heard of him since he graduated high school and went away to college."

"How old was he when he worked here?"

"Oh, seventeen . . . eighteen maybe. He worked in back takin' donations and pricin' things. But his favorite job was stockin' shelves . . . that's when he could talk to customers. And if you know Jerome, he loves to talk and make friends!"

Jessa smiled, "I can just see it." She had to get to the bottom of Jerome's story. It helped that this lady was a talker herself. "Do you know anything about his college experience?"

"Not really. I think he was studyin' to be a geologist like his father. That's all I know."

"Did you hear anything about him helping a lady in need?" Jessa said fishing.

"Baby, he helped people in need every day here at the store!"

"I know, but . . . well, never mind." *I guess she doesn't know that part of the story.* "My name's Jessa, by the way, and your name is?"

"It's Trisha. Say, thanks for stoppin' in, Jessa. I better stop gabbing and get to work. But if there's anything else I can do for you, let me know!"

"Thanks. There's one thing you may be able to help me with. It's a long story, but I . . . Jerome is a special person, and I want to know more about . . . well, I'm trying to meet more people around here who know him, if that makes any sense."

"Oh," Trisha said with an amused look on her face.

"I have been talking to a lot of people, and no one seems to know his story about why he quit college."

"He quit? I didn't know that!"

Jessa wondered if she had made the mistake of giving the small town's news lady something new to "gab" about. "Do you know any of his family or friends in the area?"

"Well . . ." her tone indicated the answer was not a straight no. . . .maybe even a yes. "I knew his father, but not very well . . . more because his name would come up in the newspaper now and then. I hear he's been out of the country for a while on business."

There went the idea of visiting the man. Jessa wasn't sure she wanted to meet him anyway.

Trisha continued. "There's Chad Hornby. He and Jerome were good friends, and I think they went to the same university."

"Do you know of a way I could connect with him?"

"Actually, I'm probably not supposed to do this, but if he has an account here at the store I should be able to pull up his information for you." Trisha walked over to the register and logged in. Within a minute she had Chad's phone number for Jessa.

Trisha waved goodbye as Jessa turned to leave a few minutes later. "Come back any time! Maybe next time you can get a cup of coffee and we can sit and chat about your discoveries!"

Maybe . . . or maybe not, Jessa thought. This lady had been friendly and helpful, but she wasn't the type to keep her mouth shut. For Jerome's sake, she didn't want the whole town gossiping about him.

Mom, I just can't figure out what God is doing in my life," Hannah lamented. "I thought Mark was the one for me. I thought we would make a great team together for the Lord. But then . . . he started loosing interest in areas of ministry. So what does God want me to do now?"

"Honey, I'm sorry," Mrs. Kallenbach said softly, sitting down next to her at the table. "I know this has all been very hard for you."

"It has, but really, Mommy, what now?"

"I don't know what God is doing in the long run, but I can give you some advice for today . . . and for tomorrow. . . . Give the day to Him, live it for Him, and through Him . . . in whatever small or great way He may ask you to. Hannah Honey, He has important things for you to do every day, no matter where you are, or whether you're married or not!"

"I know that's true, Mom. But besides my dream of getting married, why has God given me the desire to be a missionary, and then crumbled all my plans of how to make that a reality? I thought Mark and I would be a great team on the mission field."

"First of all," her mother began, "you can still be a missionary without marrying Mark." She winked at her daughter.

"Yes, I know, but . . ."

"God could still open doors for you to go to a foreign field, or . . . He may want you to do mission work *right here* at home! Just think, Hannah, how many souls there are here in our hometown that need to be saved! No matter where you are, there is missionary work to be done. Perhaps this is just a training ground for another mission field God has in mind for your future. Whatever happens, I just want you to know how important this time in your life is. It's a training ground. God is teaching you something amazing . . . probably many things. Can you think of anything specific He's been showing you through all of this?"

Hannah stared thoughtfully, rubbing the palm of her hand. "I guess He's been teaching me to trust Him more . . . to just let go of my plans and be okay with His. It's not easy though. And I've had to ask myself, 'Am I willing to give up my dream of marrying and moving away to a foreign mission field?' In my heart, I think I am willing, but another part of me wants to hang on."

"Hannah, it's not necessarily that God will never fulfill that dream. Perhaps He is the One who gave you that desire in the first place. But He may be testing you to see if you're willing to give it up for Him."

Hannah looked up as she began to understand the concept her mother was laying out. "Kind of like God tested Abraham when He told him to sacrifice Isaac . . . ."

"Yes," Mrs. Kallenbach said in a gentle voice. "God asked him to do something more difficult than giving up his own life – giving up his son's life. When Abraham came to the point where he was willing and ready to do it, God told him he didn't actually have to.

"I've seen God use this pattern many times in my own life. He gives me a desire, then He closes all the doors and says 'No.' It isn't until after I completely let go and submit that desire to Him that He opens the doors and fulfills that desire in my life."

"I know. I'm trying to submit my desires to Him and find joy simply in following His will one day at a time."

"I'm praying for you, Honey," her mother said standing up and giving her a squeeze on the shoulders. "And I talked to Grace today while you were in town. She said to give you her love and tell you she's praying a lot for you."

"She is?" Hannah looked up with light in her eyes. "I thought she'd be too occupied . . . ."

"You're one of her best friends, Hannah! She hasn't spent as much time here since the wedding, but that's to be expected. Even so, she's not going to forget about you!"

"Thanks, Mommy," Hannah said standing up. "I think I'll go up and read my Bible for a while."

Chapter Five

*I*t was nearing the middle of July - five weeks since Mark had come to Denver. Five weeks since meeting Jerome. Five weeks since landing at the Wanbli's hotel. Elu and Shawna Wanbli had become his friends. They were the best people to work for, and Mark felt accepted as one of the family. Elu was a man with an unusual blend of compassion and logic. He ran his business well, giving heed to important details, finances and necessities. Just as much, he made provision for helping those in need. A plaque on the wall of the hotel lobby read, *And now abideth faith, hope, charity, these three; but the greatest of these is charity. 1 Corinthians 13:13* The Wanbli's seemed to instill in their children every day the importance of that God-like love, charity.

"Mark," Elu's voice floated in from the hallway.

Mark set his paint roller down in the tray. "I'm in here painting."

Elu came in and surveyed Mark's progress on the walls. Each block of five rooms had a different theme. There were the Ocean Rooms, the Log Cabin Rooms, the Prairie Rooms, the Victorian Rooms.... Mark loved how much character this place had! Several rooms needed new paint, so Elu had asked Mark to tackle the job.

"It's looking great!" he said after surveying the room.

"Thanks!"

"Shawna told me about your friend Jerome. She said he's been staying in a tent and eating at McDonald's?"

Mark chuckled. "Yeah, he seems to be doing alright though."

"Okay. But if you want to let him stay with you in the Forest Room, my wife and I are okay with that."

"With no charge to him?"

"No charge," Elu said confidently. "You are already paying for the room with your help here, like we talked about. It doesn't make a whole lot of difference whether it's one or two staying in the room."

"Wow! That's kind of you, Elu. Thanks! I'll talk to Jerome and see what he says."

"He would have to pay for any meals he eats here, of course."

"Right. And I'm sure if he stays here he'll eat here quite a bit. He's got to be getting tired of McDonald's!" Mark laughed.

"Well, you talk to him and let me know what he says." Elu tapped the edge of the door and left with a smile.

The sound of crunching gravel was heard outside as a big blue Dodge Ram pickup pulled into the Kallenbach driveway.

"Somebody's here!" Joey announced, looking out the window. "A guy's getting out . . . who is that?"

Hannah took a quick look. "Oh, I think that's the Jasper guy that works at the grocery store, isn't it? Remember? He found out from Daniel that we have church at our house, and showed up a couple weeks ago."

"Yeah, you're right! I wonder what he's doing here?"

Mr. Kallenbach met him at the door.

The man greeted him like an awkward long-time friend. "Hi Ben! It's great to see you again! I was driving right by your house so thought I'd stop by."

Mr. Kallenbach stepped outside and closed the door behind him. He didn't think his family really cared to visit with this friendly stranger just now. It had been quite obvious during their first introduction at church that this 40-some-year-old guy was wife-hunting. His passion was racing cars and playing video games. Oh, and eating good food. *That's* why he needed a wife, he said, and also to do the housework and help him on his "down days" when he needed someone to console him.

Ben Kallenbach kindly carried on conversation, wondering if this was really a good use of his time. Jasper seemed as if he had all the time in the world.

An hour later, Hannah and the younger siblings checked out the window and Jasper was showing their dad all the gadgets on his new truck. "Poor Dad!" Tyler said shaking his head.

After what seemed like hours, the sound of the truck engine starting could be heard from inside. "Oh good. He's leaving," Mrs. Kallenbach said.

"I think he's just giving Dad a ride in his truck!" Joey observed. "Can I go too, Mom?!"

"No, just stay inside right now."

Jasper spun the truck's tires on the gravel as they took off, leaving a cloud of dust in the Kallenbachs' driveway. Hannah tried not to roll her eyes. This guy acted like he was eighteen, not forty. And who did he think he was impressing anyway?

When the truck returned a few minutes later, Mr. Kallenbach got out, cordially said "Goodbye" and went into the house. The rest of the family was huddled around the door waiting to hear a report from him when he came in.

"Guess what he asked me about within the first five minutes of our conversation . . . and then again fifteen minutes later, and again in the truck . . . and again when I got out of the truck?"

"Was he asking about Hannah?" Mrs. Kallenback asked incredulously.

"Yup. He says he's been getting all sort of dates through a dating site, but none of the gals want to go out with him more than twice!"

"I wonder why?" Hannah said sarcastically. "Thanks, Dad, for turning him away. There are a million reasons I would never marry him."

"The guy . . . he coming back." Seth, who was standing by the window, informed.

Joey went to look out the window, Heather Rose following right behind him. "Me look, Joy? Me look, Joy?" She said holding up her hands for Joey to help her see out the window. "Yeah, his truck is still out there," he confirmed after picking up his little sister. "And he's walking up to the door!"

Mr. Kallenbach stepped outside again.

Daniel sighed with a serious face, looking at his siblings and mother. "Sorry I told him where we live, Guys. I thought it was okay 'cause he sounded like he maybe wanted to come to our church. He asked where we meet, so I told him how we have church in homes and usually meet at our house."

"It's okay," his mom assured him. "Next time, though, it might be better to just give out our phone number if a stranger is interested in our home church. Then they can call, and Dad can give them more information."

A few minutes later Mr. Kallenbach came in with another report. "You're not going to believe this. One of the aftermarket steering shafts on his truck is completely broken.

Probably all those fast corners he took me on a few minutes ago! He's not going anywhere now."

There was a surprised murmur across the room.

"I can help fix it, Dad!" Daniel offered. He was only fourteen but enjoyed learning all he could about mechanics. "We'll probably need to get some parts in town," he surmised after a moment. "Guys, I think this project is going to take a while."

"Well," Mr. Kallenbach said with a chuckle, "looks like we're going to have a guest for dinner!"

Enjoying a hearty breakfast of scrambled eggs, pancakes and bacon, Mark observed the others in the hotel dining area. He always enjoyed the delicious meals provided at the Wanbli's diner. The five lively Wanbli children sat at the larger table by the window having breakfast. This hotel and diner was their home. Overall they were well-mannered, but once in a while a little uncharitable ruckus would erupt. "Sam, you already had enough raisins! Why did you go get more?" Adella, the oldest of them, scolded. She was only nine years old, but she often took it upon herself to act as "mother" when the younger ones were misbehaving.

Five-year-old Sam had a ready excuse. "The other raisins were teeny! Like one of them was, like, the size of a fruit fly!"

Mark tried not to chuckle out loud.

"Fruit flies . . . entirely unappetizing!" Someone muttered as they entered the room. Mark looked up to see the newcomer.

"Good morning," Mrs. Wanbli greeted Richard Keller as he surveyed the dining area. She distractedly set a glass of milk down on the table in front of her three year old, Daisy. Then she proceeded to make their new guest comfortable. "Have a seat anywhere you like. Mark over there might enjoy some company."

Mark gestured invitingly for him to sit down. The two greeted each other and began to get acquainted over breakfast.

Mark glanced over at the loud distraction the children were making. Daisy had spilled her milk all over the table and carpet. Mark got up and helped clean up the mess.

"Ah, kids!" He said smiling as he rejoined the businessman at the other table. "They sure do keep you entertained!"

"That's one word for it, but I think I'd describe it more as distracted from life. When you have kids, you can't get anything done!"

"Well, I guess the way we view it depends on what our priorities are," Mark said humbly.

"I had two of my own," Richard Keller said, cutting up his pancake, "And I couldn't wait for them to be on their own in this world, making a living, giving me something to be proud of them for. My son has done a fine job of it, but my daughter . . . not so much. She has a mind of her own."

Pressing Toward the Mark

Mark kept his thoughts unspoken. *How sad to view children as a burden like that... to think the way they pay you back is by making you proud by their worldly success!* Mark loved children, and hoped to have some of his own someday.

As he sat thinking, Jerome came in quietly with a paper bag behind his back. He was always up to something. Tiptoeing up behind Mark, he suddenly dropped the bag over his head and ran out of the room. "Good morning to you too, Jerome," Mark said, taking the bag off of his head. Jerome appeared again and sat down at the table.

"Jerome, this is our newest guest here at the hotel, Mr... I'm sorry, I guess I never asked your name," he said addressing Richard Keller.

"Ah," he hesitated, "It's Rick. Just call me Rick."

"Pleasure to meet ya, Sir," Jerome greeted, holding out his hand.

Richard Keller eyed Jerome suspiciously. "Likewise, Young Man...." His words were drawn out and as he said them he squeezed Jerome's hand so hard that he was half a second away from letting out a yelp!

When Jerome had recovered from the handshake he went on telling Rick how Mark was the hotel handyman, and that he was... well, just the handyman's roommate.

After breakfast, Jerome and Mark headed to their favorite rock climbing spot. What they did not realize was that someone else was following close behind.

Pressing Toward the Mark

Jessa's grandmother set two glasses of freshly squeezed orange juice on the table. "There we go, Darlin'," she said in her thick Georgia accent. "Something fresh an' sweet to brighten your heart! Like I always say, it's good for body *and* soul!"

Jessa loved this sweet woman. After spending several days in Jerome's hometown and not finding satisfactory answers, she had headed further south to see her grandma. "Thanks, Mamaw." She slid a glass toward herself and took a sip.

"Now," the older lady said getting down to business, "you've told me your story, and I've had a little time to think about it. Makin' orange juice is as good an excuse as any to step away and churn up some wisdom," she said with a wink.

"What's your wise counsel for me this time?" The combination of the orange juice and the company of her grandma was helping already.

"When your daddy came askin' for your momma, well, it was hard for your papaw and me. He came from a wealthy family, was already established as CEO of his company, and had big dreams for his career. We worried it was too much of his focus. But our daughter had fallen in love with him and wouldn't hear our precautions. We wanted to accept him lovingly too . . . for her sake. And so, we gave them our blessing to be married. Now I see some of the heartache that has resulted over the years. I don't want to continue going back and saying 'we should have this or that' because it's done and over now. But now I ask myself, what can I learn through this? One thing I've learned is how important it is to ask some questions when you find yourself 'fallin' in love' with somebody."

"What kind of questions?"

"Like . . . What does this man believe? Do we have the same views on life, and God, and family? Will he be a good, faithful husband and father? Do I really want to spend the rest of my life with him, or am I just feelin' the rush of emotions and hormones and such that can come and go?"

"You're so serious, Mamaw," Jessa said whipping the lock of blonde hair out of her face.

"Relationships are serious . . . 'specially life long ones like marriage!"

"Yeah . . . ."

"Honey, is Jesus important to you?"

"Of course."

"And why?"

"Well . . ." Jessa shifted uncomfortably in her chair, "you know . . . He's God."

"That's right. And He's your Savior! Is Jerome a Christian?"

"I'm . . . not exactly sure. We haven't really talked about it much. I guess he'd call himself agnostic."

Mamaw raised one eyebrow.

"But Mamaw, he and I are very understanding of each other, and this hasn't been a problem at all."

"Jessa, do you know what 2 Corinthians 6:14 says?" Mamaw picked up her Bible from the counter and flipped to the passage. *"Be ye not unequally yoked together with unbelievers: for what fellowship hath righteousness with unrighteousness? and what communion hath light with darkness?* Is there a closer human relationship or 'yoke' than that of marriage?"

"I guess not."

"Now, I don't agree with some of your father's requirements for the man you marry. I don't think it's important for your man to have popularity and a high payin' job. But I do see a problem if the man you're considering is not a believer." She could see on her granddaughter's face that she had a lot of thoughts to sort out. "Sweetie, go home. Give yourself time to think and pray earnestly about this."

"Got somthin' for you to fill out," Jerome said confidently, slipping a form onto the table in front of Mark.

"What's this?"

"Passport application," Jerome replied, watching Mark's expression, while adjusting his tie-dyed sweatband.

"For what?" Mark held up the form, looking quizzically at it and then at his friend.

Pressing Toward the Mark

"You know," Jerome said, taking a seat across the table from him, "there is a world of adventure out there just waiting for you to enjoy it! I know you've traveled a bit around the States, but what about other countries?"

"Yeah, but Jerome," Mark tried to protest, but his friend had more to say.

"I was thinking we should take a trip sometime to Kalymnos, Greece." Jerome's eyes shone with exuberance. "I've been dreaming of all the rock climbing expeditions we could do there. Kalymnos is like, Europe's epicenter for rock climbing. Just think, Mark! Hundreds of climbing routes, lots of sun, beautiful Mediterranean weather, and amazing geological history on top of it all. I can just see us there, climbing those limestone cliffs!"

Mark hesitated. "Greece? I'm not sure, Jerome. I'm not quite as adventurous as you are."

"Well, we wouldn't have to go to Greece necessarily. I just think you should do some traveling, and I would love a rock climbing companion on my next international expedition. Just fill out the form so you can get your passport, and be ready when an opportunity comes up!"

"Okay," Mark agreed, sighing. "But I'm not making any promises that I'll go with you."

"Fair enough," Jerome said, getting up to leave. "You'll thank me later."

Pressing Toward the Mark

Mark looked at his watch again. *How did we get ourselves into this?* The afternoon had dragged on as he and Jerome followed Mr. Keller all over the golf course. Bored? That was an understatement! Though the older gentleman had tried to explain the rules of the game, they still followed clueless with clubs in hand, wondering how much longer they would have to stay. Mr. Keller asked questions here and there which kept some conversation going. Since Jerome loved to tell his stories, just one question would keep him rambling for about 15 minutes. This was exactly what Richard Keller hoped to accomplish in the afternoon outing. To learn more about Jerome. Mark wanted to learn a little bit about Rick too. What was his background? What was his family like? What brought him to Colorado for two weeks? And why did he care to spend time with him and Jerome?

"So, Rick, what brings you to Denver?"

"Ahhh . . . beautiful," he said tracing the path his golf ball took through the air. He hadn't forgotten the question though. "Just a couple of business conferences I am speaking at. I had the trip planned a long way in advance . . . I just didn't expect . . . well anyway, what brings each of you here?"

Jerome was the first to answer. "This is just one of my stops on my journey to explore the world, Rick," he said picking up his golf club and spinning around with his arms outstretched to the view surrounding them.

Something about Jerome's free and humorous spirit made Richard Keller want to chuckle, but he had long before this trip decided that Jerome was a loser who had no right to his daughter. Yes, Jessa would marry someone with a college education and a high paying job. He pushed away the spark of

Pressing Toward the Mark

liking he had for Jerome and resorted to his stiff business composure. "What about you, Mark?"

"Ah, well . . . ." How was he to answer that? He didn't know the man well enough to explain his reasons. He hadn't even told Jerome about it yet. "It's sort of a needed, last minute vacation for me."

After a seemingly unending afternoon, the men returned to the hotel. Mr. Keller went to his room puzzled. *If Jerome has really run off with my daughter, then where is she? Why have there been no signs of her? If she were in the area, surely they would be rock climbing together.* Maybe Jessa did go to Georgia like she said. He let out a huff of air. *I have a lot of important business to focus on during this trip. When I get home, I'll track down my daughter and get to the bottom of this.*

That afternoon, Mark and Jerome packed a few things and headed up to one of Jerome's favorite camping spots in the mountains.

"Glad you agreed to camp with me for a few nights," the adventurer said pounding in the last tent stake. "Don't you just feel like out here you're *really* living?" Jerome stood up and drew in a deep breath of mountain air.

Mark nodded in agreement, gazing out over the lofty view.

"Hotels are okay and everything, but it's so much more of an adventure to be out in nature!" Jerome paused like a little boy in trouble and glanced in Mark's direction. "Not that I'm ungrateful to you for letting me stay in your hotel room!" Sometimes he wished he had better control over what came out of his mouth.

As the sun sunk behind the horizon, Mark built a small campfire. Jerome sat, watching him with amusement.

Mark's mind was focused on the question Rick Keller had asked earlier that day. It was time to tell Jerome why he had left Indiana. "I haven't really told you why I came here, Jerome," he said, focusing on the burning twig he was using to light more of the fire.

Jerome tried to read the look on Mark's face. "Runnin' away from somethin'?"

"In a way...." Mark sat down, joining his friend on the hard ground. "Less than two months ago I was in a relationship with the most beautiful, godly young lady I've ever met. I was going to ask her to marry me. But then . . . well, I guess I wasn't good enough for her." As he spoke those words, he felt even more sorry for himself.

Jerome listened with a serious face as Mark explained the details of that heartbreaking day of his sister's wedding. He purposely evaded the part about his lack of passion for evangelism, and Hannah's desire to be a missionary. It just seemed more and more awkward to talk with Jerome about those things as time went on. Besides, he didn't want to offend his friend by pushing religious stuff on him. Deep down in his heart though, Mark knew this was the very issue that kept Hannah from marrying him.

Chapter Six

"Hi Jessa, this is Chad Hornby." Jessa's mind focused when she heard that name over the phone. "I'm sorry for not returning your calls earlier. You said you are a friend of Jerome from California?"

"Yes, thank you for calling me back." She then told him briefly what she was looking for and why.

"Interesting," he said when she had concluded. "Trisha is right. Jerome and I were good friends. We roomed together in college, until he dropped out."

"See, that's the part I don't understand!" Jessa interrupted. "What was his reason for dropping out?"

"I don't know the whole story, but I know a lady called Mrs. Malloy had to do with it. She's a widow who lives here in Medford, where Jerome and I went to college. She has one son who ran away into the military and never writes or calls. Jerome met her one day as she was trying to carry her groceries home from the store. He could see she was having a terrible time of it and offered to help. It turns out she had congestive heart failure and needed to see a doctor. The next day, something led Jerome to stop by her house to check on her. She was doing so poorly that he ended up bringing her to the hospital."

"Wow!" Jessa commented.

"Jerome felt bad for her and for several weeks spent a lot of time with her at the hospital. I was surprised when he failed his finals for that semester. He was always an above-average student growing up. He never really explained to me what was going on. He just packed up after that and told me he was going to California."

"Thanks for sharing this with me. It helps a lot. Do you know how I can get in touch with Mrs. Malloy? I'd like to hear the story from her."

"Yes. I know where she lives, but she might not want me to give that information out to a stranger." There was a short silence on his end of the phone. "I guess I can stop by there this afternoon and see if she'd like to meet with you. When would you be available?"

"Umm . . . ." Jessa had to think about logistics. She was in southern Georgia at the moment with her grandma, but she could be to Medford Georgia by the next afternoon. "I could meet her tomorrow afternoon or the next day."

"Okay. I'll let you know what she says."

The next afternoon Jessa found herself seated on Mrs. Malloy's old, lime-green sofa with a glass of sweet tea in her hand. After explaining her mission, she asked Mrs. Malloy for her story about Jerome.

"He has such a tender heart," Mrs. Malloy said, patting her hand on her heart. "He couldn't stand leaving me all alone at the hospital, facing multiple heart surgeries. So he spent as much time there with me as he could. All of this happened at the end of the semester, so he needed to be studying for finals. But he said even when he went home, he couldn't focus to study. I felt like it was my fault, but he told me not to worry. Finals came and went and he failed. He wasn't used to failing in school, and he didn't know how to respond to this. Jerome supported me through all three of my surgeries, and then shocked me with the news that he was moving to California."

"That's where I met him. I'm from California," Jessa interjected. "But please, continue. I want to hear more."

"I felt so bad that he failed in college because of me. And at first, I didn't understand why he had to leave . . . but as time went on, I heard people here in the town talking. People *love* to talk you know. When Jerome came to say goodbye, I asked him straight out why he was leaving. He explained it all to me. As you probably know, his father is a well-known geologist and very proud of his own accomplishments. He always wanted Jerome to follow in his steps. He was happy when Jerome showed interest in pursuing the same career and funded all of his son's tuition. That lasted two years, until Jerome failed that one semester. Jerome's dad was quick to tell people how ashamed he was of his son and how he would not give another penny to pay for tuition that would simply be wasted. Even though he knew about Jerome helping me, he didn't see why that was any excuse for his son to fail classes. I think Jerome just lost heart when his dad responded this way.... He wanted to get away from all the gossip, and his dad's constant degrading. He felt like everyone in the area viewed him as a failure and a looser. He wanted to get a fresh start and make a good name for himself."

Jessa sat quietly soaking in everything Mrs. Malloy said. It all started to make sense in her mind. The missing piece of the puzzle fit. Just like she thought, Jerome was not a loser. Now she couldn't wait to head back to California and prove it to her father.

The recorded squaky-voiced singing seemed to come from nowhere. "Old McDonald had a farm, E I E I O!" Mr. Keller, trying to eat his late breakfast, was getting annoyed with the incessant noise. He got up and started looking for the source. Soon he spotted the little green flip phone sitting on a chair. He picked it up, wondering why anyone would have such an absurd ring tone, pushed the off button, and set it back down. Then he paused. This was the place Jerome always sat when he came to breakfast with Mark. He grabbed the phone once again and slipped it into his pocket.

Pressing Toward the Mark

As he sat finishing his breakfast, he was deep in thought, analyzing his recent interactions with Jerome. He was still determined to despise the young man.

Mr. Keller just about jumped out of his seat when the loud sound of a frog croaking came from very near by! "What in the world!" he said, feeling a vibration in his chest pocket and realizing the croaking had come from the same place. Digging into his pocket, he pulled out the green "frog."

"Ah!" he shouted throwing it out of his hands. When it hit the floor, he realized the "frog" was Jerome's phone. Feeling quite fooled, he picked it up, and read the new text that the "frog" had been announcing. He was not ready for what it said.

"Jerome, I really need you right now. I'm in Alabama and I've been in a bad car accident. Please come! I'm at Southwestern Memorial Hospital. ~Jessa"

"NO!" Mr. Keller shouted out loud. *I am the one she needs right now, not that good for nothing boyfriend!*

"Jessa," her father began to write back,

"I won't be coming. Things have changed, and my feelings for you are not as they used to be. I'm sending your dad. Follow doctors' orders and I'm sure you'll be up and around again in no time. All the best to you. ~Jerome"

With shaky hands he hit the send button and then placed the phone into the lost and found basket sitting at the deserted front desk.

Pressing Toward the Mark

"Alright, Mr. Keller," the hospital receptionist said, glancing up from her computer. "Your daughter is in room number 244."

Richard nodded and headed in the direction of the elevator. As the elevator brought him to the second floor he fidgeted nervously with his hands in his pockets. *Jessa has to pull through this! We need to get our lives back together and start fresh. I wonder how she will respond to me coming instead of Jerome. She should have been asking for me anyway.*

He stepped out of the elevator, located the Intensive Care Unit and identified his daughter's room.

A kind, young nurse escorted him in. "Good morning, Jessa. Someone is here to see you."

"Dad?" Jessa tried to lift her head but the pain restrained her.

"Honey, I'm so glad you're okay! I came as soon as I could!"

"Why are you here? Did Jerome really send you?"

"Of course, Honey! You're my only daughter and you've just been in an accident. What kind of father would I be in the eyes of . . . well anyone, if I wasn't here for you? And Jerome . . . he's already told you where he stands, and it's obvious by my presence here instead of him."

Pressing Toward the Mark

"But Dad, I need him right now!"

"You need ME right now! That immature wander-foot has caused us all enough problems already. Come on, Honey, why don't you tell me about your accident."

Jessa looked with self-pity toward the window. "I wouldn't even have been in an accident if you hadn't tried so hard to push your way on me. From the very beginning you never accepted Jerome just because he wasn't rich and didn't come from a political, well-known family."

"It was all for your sake, Jessa. Ten years from now you'll thank me. What kind of life would it be, traveling around to who knows where, rock climbing and having picnics for the rest of your life! What about a career? What about a name for yourself? What about all the things that matter in life?"

"*People* matter more than things, Dad! And I'd rather live my whole life rock climbing with the person I love than living in a stuck-up neighborhood with a house full of things that could never make me happy!"

Neither of them spoke as those words rang in Richard's mind. Then Jessa started again. "Jerome didn't mean what he said. I know him, and I know he really cares for me. He probably said what he said and told you where I was just because you scared and threatened him into it. Jerome might not be the bravest man ever, but he really loves and cares about people . . . and I'm surprised he sent that text, even if he didn't mean it."

"Look, Jessa," Richard said, his cheeks turning red, "I didn't come here to talk about Jerome. What he said and did is done and settled. I came because you're in the hospital, and we need to work together on getting you better."

The young nurse came in and checked Jessa's vitals. Richard introduced himself as her father, and then began to ask questions about his daughter's condition.

Jessa closed her eyes, trying to interpret the mix of strange emotions within her. Something didn't feel right. A deep sense of sadness overcame her. It wasn't just the text from Jerome. It wasn't that her dad wouldn't accept him. Jerome was in some sort of trouble. She just knew.

Kneeling down beside Jerome's backpack, Mark began to pull out its contents and lay the things in a pile on the hospital room floor. Jerome was out of surgery now, but the doctors were keeping him sedated and paralyzed while they continued to monitor the pressure on his brain.

His cell phone must be in here somewhere, Mark thought. *I need to look up some of his contacts from back home in Georgia . . . a family member or something to let them know what's happened!* Upon reaching the bottom he found a photo. On the back was written the name: *Jessa Keller.* "So this is your Jessa," he said with a half smile and glancing over toward his friend's bed. "She has that same mischievous smile that you do. She needs to know what's happened to you too, but how can I tell her without getting her number from your phone?" He looked at the name again. *Jessa Keller . . . Rick Keller . . . . Is Rick her father? Why would I even think that?*

Pressing Toward the Mark

But she does look a little like him, doesn't she? There has to be a reason why Mr. Keller has taken such interest in Jerome these past weeks and asked so many questions. Maybe Rick thinks Jerome knows where Jessa is.

Mark set the photo down next to the pile of Jerome's belongings and sat in the chair next to the hospital bed. Jerome's beloved bandana lay on the nightstand near him. A tear welled up in one eye and Mark's chest burned inside him. He watched his friend lie perfectly still with no sign of consciousness. "How could I be so selfish! How could I be so foolish not to tell you about the Lord? I'm sorry, Man. Please wake up so I can tell you the Good News that I've kept from you all this time!"

The day was a long one. Mark sat in the waiting room, wishing for at least a little piece of good news. But as the hours dragged on, the news on Jerome seemed only to be getting worse.

That evening, as the last bit of sunlight disappeared, the doctor called for Mark. Jerome had taken his last breath. He was gone.

Richard Keller answered the phone apprehensively. "Hello?"

"Rick, this is Mark Evans . . . from the hotel in Denver."

"Yes, Mark, what can I do for you?"

"You remember Jerome, right?"

Mr. Keller's face began to feel hot and sweaty at the mention of that name. "Yes, of course."

"Well, I was going to tell you this when I saw you at the hotel next, but Mrs. Wanbli said you had left in a hurry and weren't planning to come back. Jerome took a bad fall when rock climbing earlier this week . . . ."

"Is he still in the hospital?"

Mark took a deep breath before answering. "No . . . . He didn't make it."

"Jerome died?" Mr. Keller's mouth dropped open.

"Yes, Sir. His funeral is in two days."

"I'm sorry, Mark . . . ."

"Me too." Mark looked out the window of his hotel room with a growing lump in his throat. "For the past few days Jerome's phone has been missing. That's actually one of the last things he talked to me about before he headed out to scale. Anyway, I've been trying to find his phone so I can get some contact information for his friends and family. I know he really doesn't have much of a family – if he did, I'd let them do the funeral planning – but I need to notify at least a few people about what's happened. Do you by any chance recall seeing his phone anywhere?"

Mr. Keller gulped and looked around nervously. The guilt in his chest seemed to be growing every second. "I . . . um . . . let me think . . . ." He ran his hand over his

Pressing Toward the Mark

graying hair. "Yes! Actually I'm pretty sure I saw it at the hotel in the lost and found basket."

"Great! I'll check there right now." Mark entered the hallway and headed downstairs to the lobby. There was silence on the phone as neither one could think of anything to say. Mark approached the front desk and looked hopefully into the lost and found basket. There it was... the very recognizable green flip-phone that belonged to Jerome... that *used to* belong to Jerome. "I found it!"

"Good."

"Thanks so much for your help, Rick." There was something more Mark wanted to ask but he didn't have a clue how to bring it up.

Mr. Keller spoke up before Mark had time to ask. "Mark, I don't know why I'm telling you this, but I feel like I should. I am Jessa's father." He paused for a second. "You knew that already, didn't you."

"I had guessed," Mark confessed. He was grateful to have the answer to his nagging curiosity. "I don't think Jerome had any idea though. Did he know your name? I mean, before he met you here in Denver?"

"Back home in California I always go by Richard. I think going by "Rick" threw him off. Mark, I didn't mean him any harm. I just wanted my daughter back."

"He and Jessa never met up here in Denver. He knew she was somewhere in Georgia, but he quit following her because he was afraid of you."

"That's what I'm gathering." Mr. Keller rubbed his forehead feeling miserable. "And Jessa swears she hasn't seen Jerome since she left California."

"So you've been in contact with her?" Mark asked.

"Yes. In fact, she was in an accident too and is in the hospital right now, on her way to recovery. I've been here to support her until she can come home."

"Okay, I'm glad you're there for her. Can you gently break the news to her about Jerome when the time is right? I'm assuming she won't be able to make it to the funeral."

"I'm sure she won't. But I will tell her."

"Thanks, Mr. Keller."

"Take care, Mark."

Mr. Keller sat down limply on the hotel room bed. He stared numbly at the floor. The one piece of deception he had run with had come back to torment him. He felt as though a glowing volcano inside him had just erupted, and its burning lava had flowed over into every part of his being, bubbling, and destroying. He had thrown such a cruel and false wrench into Jessa and Jerome's relationship, and now, Jerome had passed away with not another chance to tell Jessa the truth about how he felt toward her.

"I'm a Christian man!" he said repentantly. "How could I be so dishonest . . . and heartless? God, I've been so wrong! I'm so sorry." He rested his face in his hands and tears began to flow. "I need to confess this to Jessa, don't I? How will she ever forgive me? I've been such a hardhearted fool! All I've cared about is my money, my reputation, and my social standing. But all this time, I've been loosing the hearts of my children. And now this! Lord, I'm such a fool!"

He lifted his head, and his gaze wandered to the nightstand next to the bed. Opening the drawer in it he found what he was looking for: a Gideon Bible. He opened it and read for quite some time. God spoke to his heart. He knew what he had to do . . . not so God would forgive him, not to be saved from hell, not to be cleansed from sin – God had already done that. He needed to tell Jessa the whole story, and ask for her forgiveness. He needed to not only *be* a Christian, but to *live* like one by doing what was right.

Funeral arrangements were not what Mark anticipated doing during his stay in Colorado, but here he was, doing exactly that. *It's a shame,* he admitted, *to think that Jerome's family is so distant and disconnected that none of them would take initiative and honor him with a memorial service! I know I'm not obligated to make any arrangements either, but it's the last thing I can do for my friend. I hope his family will at least make an appearance at the funeral.* How Mark grieved the death of his lively friend whom he had met less than three months earlier. He was realizing more and more how complicated life can be. One day planning to marry the love of his heart, the next, having that dream torn away, then starting over in a new place, and finding something completely different to occupy his mind and time. As Mark mused upon the events of the past weeks of Jerome's life, something didn't add up. *That text I saw when I was looking for contacts on his phone... why would he have said that to Jessa? As far as I could tell, he still loved her. Wait. When was that text sent?* A second look at Jerome's phone revealed that it was the most recent text and was dated August 10th. *That's the day Jerome and I went camping. On the 9th, he had mentioned that he couldn't find his phone, so we went camping without it. The phone was missing until Mr. Keller told me he had seen it in the lost and found box.... Someone other than Jerome had to have sent that text.* Mark squeezed his eyes shut and shook his head as the pieces came together. *Could Richard Keller be that heartless?*

Chapter Seven

Six year old Willie Kallenbach hurried in the direction of the ringing cell phone sitting on the dining room table. Grace was visiting and had left her phone inside while she went out to help in the garden.

"Hello?"

Mark paused and listened to the shuffling sounds on the other end of the line as Willie tried to push the speaker phone button. "Hi, this is Mark, who is this?" he said, guessing it was one of the Kallenbach children.

"Willie," answered the smiling boy.

"Hi Willie! How are you?"

"Good. Grace is outside working in the garden."

"Okay, can you tell her I called?"

Pressing Toward the Mark

"Yeah." Willie's answers were short, but his face showed a look of *"This grown-up guy is amazing, and it's so cool I get to talk to him on the phone!"*

"Thanks! So how is everything with your family?"

"Good." Suddenly Willie's face lit up as he realized he had an interesting piece of news to share. "This guy named Jasper came to our house and he wants to marry Hannah!"

"Really?" Mark didn't know what to say.

"Yeah, he has a really cool truck, but it broke while he was here so he stayed for supper while Daniel and Joey fixed it. He talked to Dad for a long time about Hannah."

"Oh . . . . How did you guys meet him?"

"He came to church a few weeks ago."

Mark was feeling more sick to his stomach the more he learned.

"Mom's calling me. Talk to you later, Alligator!" Willie said ending the conversation.

Mark sat looking dejectedly out the window. So now Hannah had someone else. A cool guy named Jasper. Probably super on fire for God, with a beefy F350 truck. Made a Toyota Camry sound pretty wimpy. It was probably a good thing he was far away in Colorado.

Pressing Toward the Mark

Jessa stared in disbelief and anger as her father left the hospital room. Could he have created a bigger, more painful mess? And after all that he had done, he expected her to forgive him. Did he have the slightest idea how those words he wrote "from Jerome" had been tearing her up from the inside out? And now Jerome was gone... or was that just another cruel lie?

Tears began to well up in her eyes. She swallowed hard, trying to withhold the torrent of tears that was about to break loose, but the grief and confusion those tears represented were too much to suppress. "God, what am I supposed to do now?" she sobbed. "How can Jerome be gone? Why didn't I die too, in the accident?" As she spoke those words, a stark question rang back in her head. *If you had died, where would you be right now?* For the first time, she wondered if heaven really was her soul's destination. She had been to church many times as a child, and her parents were Christian... so of course she was too! But was that all there was to it? *If you had died, where would you be right now?* The question came again. "Lord," she pleaded, "I really don't understand much of the Bible, even though I've been to church a lot. How can I know for sure that I'll go to heaven? I don't want to go to hell. I'm not perfect... but have I been good enough for you to forgive me in the areas I've messed up?" She shook her head. "I'm so confused. Please help me, God."

The sun was setting and the room growing dim. Jessa flipped on the lamp next to her bed. Her father had left a Bible on the nightstand. She picked it up and began to read in the Psalms.

Pressing Toward the Mark

I waited patiently for the LORD; and he inclined unto me, and heard my cry.

He brought me up also out of an horrible pit, out of the miry clay, and set my feet upon a rock, and established my goings.

And he hath put a new song in my mouth, even praise unto our God: many shall see it, and fear, and shall trust in the LORD.

Blessed is that man that maketh the LORD his trust . . . .

Psalm 40:1-4a

Hope flooded Jessa's heart as she read these life-giving words. God would come through. He would show her the way.

Grace and Hannah found themselves absorbed in pleasant conversation as they worked together weeding carrots. It was a tedious job, but with good company they didn't mind at all. The two young ladies had been best friends, and they were both glad that Grace and her new husband lived close enough to visit often. Since she didn't have children of her own just yet, Grace had a lot of time to reach out and be a blessing to others. The Kallenbachs always appreciated when she would help on the farm – a ministry she had started before she was married.

"So it's been almost three months since Mark left," Grace commented. "How are you doing with all that's happened?"

"To be honest, Grace, God is giving me amazing peace. Letting go of Mark was really hard, but I'm confident it was what God wanted me to do. There's nothing more rewarding than following the Lord, even when it's painful."

"You're right, and I'm glad to hear you say that."

"Sometimes I'm tempted to think I was foolish to break off the relationship... because your brother is a great guy! He was just showing weakness in a particular area. Maybe I shouldn't be so picky... just settle for less, you know? I mean, will I ever find someone better? No one's perfect. I know that's not the way I should think. I know God has a beautiful plan for my life. Making compromises is simply a lack of faith on my part."

Grace shifted herself up the carrot row to reach the next weedy section. "Even though Mark's my brother, I wholeheartedly agree with you. I think his lack of enthusiasm for sharing the gospel is a big problem right now. When you commit to marry a man, you want to be sure that he will be a godly leader for your home and family. You want a man who loves the Lord more than his own life, or even you!" She looked up with a twinkle in her eye. "Hannah, you're my best friend, other than Zack, of course, and I want to see you marry someone worthy of you."

"And you don't think Mark's worthy of me?" Hannah asked softly. "Am I worthy of him?"

"I think you are worthy of him, yes. But right now I don't think he quite deserves you. I'm not saying that Mark will never be worthy of you. God can change his heart. And maybe God will bring the two of you together again someday."

Pressing Toward the Mark

Hannah stared thoughtfully at the dirt on her hands. Grace had hope for her and Mark. Maybe she should too. But she couldn't go on indefinitely, hanging on to something God led her to give up. *Lord, I put this into your hands. Mark is Yours, and so am I. Do with us as You please, even if that means leading us in different directions.*

The days after Jerome's funeral seemed to drag on. Mark continued to work for the Wanbli family around the hotel. One morning as he busied himself installing a new air conditioning unit, the sun came out from behind the clouds and beamed into the room. *Ah, it's nice to see the sun! Haven't seen it much since Jerome died*, he mused. The warm sunlight seemed to lead his mind into deep thought. He began to pray – something he hadn't done much of in the last few months. *Lord, what now? This has been such a difficult and strange summer. I've lost Hannah. And now I've lost Jerome forever. I've been so wrong. If I had been seeking You as I should have, things would have turned out differently.* Now that he started praying, he realized he had a lot to talk to God about. He walked over to the hotel room door, closed it, and got on his knees for a private, long overdue conversation with the Lord.

As he prayed, a verse came to mind that he had memorized the previous winter, Philippians 3:14. *I press toward the mark for the prize of the high calling of God in Christ Jesus.* Had he been "pressing toward the mark" or had he simply been taking his salvation for granted, and not walking according to God's design for a Christian? Mark thought about the many

Christians he knew who were living no different from the sinful world around them. Were they going to heaven? Yes. But would they one day obtain that "prize" or reward referred to in Philippians? Probably not. The stinging reality that surged through his heart now was that *he* was among that majority of lukewarm Christians. As he thought about all that Christ had done for him, saving him from an eternity in hell, shame and godly sorrow flooded over him. *And I've thanked You by being a petty coward of a Christian. I'm so sorry, Lord!* It wasn't too late to change. He had wasted some time. He had lost ground. He had fallen behind in the race. But his God was stepping along side him to help him get him back in the race. He could still fight a good fight and finish the course, by God's grace.

Many minutes later as Mark rose to his feet, he felt like a renewed man. He felt the joy of God's forgiveness. He could see clearly what he needed to do, and he felt courage from the Lord to do it. In the recent months, he had not only failed God, but he had also failed to be a true friend to Jerome by not sharing the Good News with him. There was nothing he could do now to fix that. But from now on he resolved by God's grace to be bold with the Gospel. He had failed Hannah as well. She was right for breaking things off, and Mark respected her now for that decision. That he would be given a second chance with Hannah was doubtful. But regardless of that, he would seek to be a true servant of the Lord, doing His work wholeheartedly. *"I press toward the mark for the prize of the high calling of God in Christ Jesus."* Mark quoted Philippians 3:14 aloud as he resumed his work on the air conditioning unit. "Lord, help me to do this for Your glory."

Pressing Toward the Mark

The next day Mark awoke to the ear-piercing sound of fire alarms. He sat up quickly, slipped on his shoes, and hurried down to the diner kitchen, still half asleep. He had learned in his lifetime that a fire alarm usually means nothing more than some smokey bacon being cooked, so he had little concern that there was actually a fire. His concern was all of their sleeping guests being woken up by a false alarm.

He encountered Elu and Shawna staggering into the hallway. They were talking about bacon too! Oh yes, now he could smell it. When the three reached the kitchen the cook ran up with a distressed face. "I'm so sorry!" he apologized. "The vent above the cook top isn't working, so I tried to cook the bacon for breakfast without it!"

"So there's no fire?" Mark wanted to make sure before canceling the fire alarms.

"No fire. Everything is fine."

Mark dashed away to shut off the obnoxious noise.

Several half asleep guests were frantically clamoring down the hallway to the lobby. Shawna stationed herself there to calm them down and send them back to bed.

When things had settled down, Mark returned to his room, exhausted though the day had just begun. He glanced over at what used to be Jerome's bed. Knowing Jerome, he probably would have slept through the whole ordeal.

Pressing Toward the Mark

Mark was pulled from his thoughts when his phone rang. It was Elu, asking if he could come down and take a look at the stove vent. Apparently the cook refused to use the cook top any more until the vent was repaired.

It was nearly 8:00 a.m. by the time Mark finished reassembling the fan for the stove vent. He quickly screwed the last piece in place. Somehow his thumb swiped across a thin edge of stainless steel, making a clear gash through his skin. He almost didn't feel it, but when it began gushing blood, he ran to find a Band Aid. Breakfast was served on time... but with only half of the bacon. The cook was just happy that the stove was ready to use in making lunch.

Mark washed the dusty grease from his hands with hot soap and water. *I am so ready to sit down for a while and have some breakfast.* As he came through the kitchen door to the dining area, he heard the phone at the front desk ringing. Shawna was struggling to open a container of yogurt with one hand while holding her youngest child in the other. "Mom!" Sam complained, "Sadie is sitting in my spot!"

"Mark, could you get the phone?" the mother asked, trying to handle everything.

Mark nodded and sprinted over to the desk. "Dinever Hotel and Diner. How can I help you this morning?"

"We're calling from Room 15. The toilet is plugged and it's starting to overflow onto the floor!" The woman sounded a bit distressed.

"I'll be right there." Mark hung up the phone and ran down the hall. He quickly stopped at the janitor closet and grabbed a plunger. As he rounded a corner, his foot caught on a piece of the old carpet that was coming loose. The sudden interruption to his momentum almost sent him to the floor. He managed to regain his balance and looked behind him to see if anyone had been watching. He tried not to feel frustrated. He had glued down this section of carpet just yesterday. Apparently, it didn't hold.

He had barely raised his hand to knock at Room 15, when the elderly lady opened the door. "My husband turned off the water supply to the toilet so it didn't flood the bathroom," she said admiringly.

"Oh, thank you," Mark said addressing the man. He then put some towels down to sop up the water that was already on the floor. Unplugging the toilet only took a minute. It was the clean-up that Mark disliked the most.

"You are so nice!" the lady said when he had finished. "I thank you so much for doing that. Here, take this orange as a tip." She smiled handing him the fruit.

Mark appreciated the gesture. He wasn't about to explain that he had completely lost his appetite. He took the orange and bid the couple good day.

By this time, breakfast was over, so there was no reason to return to the dining room. He meandered back to his room tossing the orange with one hand and catching it with the other. He remembered the days he used to juggle for fun. He had become quite skilled at it.

Further down the hall he passed the Wanbli's room. He could hear voices behind the door. Sounded like somebody was overtired. Maybe the fire alarms woke the kids up too early this morning. Still, it was not a good excuse for naughtiness. He could hear Shawna's calm voice. She was doing her best to discipline and love her quarreling, whining children.

Is the rest of the day going to be like this? Mark mused. *It's been a difficult day so far, but we can still chose to have good attitudes. Besides, the more grumpy everyone around me is, the more important it is for me to be joyful! This is the day which the LORD hath made. I will rejoice and be glad in it.* He laughed gently as he reflected. The morning had been so hectic, it was *almost* funny.

Chapter Eight

The forest green Toyota Camry was on the road heading east for another long trip. Mark had taken a number of great trips in this car. As he neared the Alabama border, he recalled the trip he had taken to visit the Kallenbah's oldest son, Charlie, and his wife, Sarah, after the birth of their first child. For that trip his car had been at full capacity; none of Charlie's siblings wanted to stay home in Indiana. Although Mark couldn't manage to take them all, Joey Kallenbach had found a way to be included without riding in the trunk (as he had suggested). That boy was a character! Mark smiled, remembering good times.

This time he had a very clear mission to accomplish in Alabama. Jessa, who was still recovering in the hospital, needed to know that Jerome didn't send that text. Even more importantly, she needed to know the gospel.

Pressing Toward the Mark

Mark expected he'd have to fight a feeling of uncomfortable nervousness as he entered a hospital for the first time since Jerome's death. But no, instead, he walked boldly to the front desk, inquired where Jessa could be found, and turned down the correct hall. Something in him was different. He had such vision and strength for the mission God had given him for today. *Thank you, Lord!*

A nurse escorted him into Jessa's room. He introduced himself as Jerome's friend from Colorado, and then began the awkward task of explaining the text. He didn't say it was her father who had sent it. After all, he couldn't prove that. But he did tell her that Jerome could not have been the text's author. To Mark's surprise, Jessa nodded knowingly as he explained, wiping tears from her cheeks.

"My dad told me," she said when Mark had concluded. "He's the one who sent the text."

"He told you?" Mark was shocked.

"Yeah," she said with a sniffle, "and he wants me to forgive him, but I don't think I can."

Mark's eyes turned downward. He pressed his lips together, nodding thoughtfully. *How can she forgive if she doesn't have the strength and forgiveness of God? This is my opportunity to share the gospel with her. God, please help me.*

"Jessa, can I ask you a question?"

"Sure."

"Have you personally experienced the unconditional, full forgiveness of God?"

There was a slight pause before she responded. "I . . . don't know for sure . . . ."

"Sometimes we face situations where humanly speaking it is impossible for us to truly forgive someone. The only way we can do it is if we've experienced God's forgiveness, and He gives us the power to forgive others. The Bible tells us that *all have sinned, and come short of the glory of God*. That includes you and me – we've all broken God's laws and done evil. We ALL need forgiveness."

"Yeah, I won't deny that." Jessa interjected.

"Do you know how to be forgiven of all your sins – past, present, and future?"

"Um . . . tell God you're sorry for your sins . . . and then try to turn your life around the best you can?"

"But what if you don't do a very good job turning your life around? How good do you have to be? You see, Jessa, so many people go through life *hoping* that the way they live will be acceptable *enough* for God so that they can go to heaven. But God's standard is perfection. No one can go to heaven unless they are *sinless*."

"So none of us are qualified, no matter how good we are . . . ." Jessa concluded.

"Right. Romans 3:10 says that *there is none righteous, no not one*." Jessa seemed to be receptive, and Mark wanted to do a thorough job of explaining salvation to her. He pulled his Bible out of his backpack and turned to Isaiah 64:6. "*But we are all as an unclean thing, and all our righteousnesses are as filthy rags; and we all do fade as a leaf; and our iniquities, like the wind, have taken us away."*

Jessa listened thoughtfully and then blurted out with a hint of desperation in her voice, "But Jesus died for our sins, so we're okay, right?" It was evident she had grown up hearing all the Christian lingo, but the words flowing off her lips seemed to carry no personal meaning to her.

"Jesus did come to die for us. 1 Timothy 1:15 says, *This is a faithful saying, and worthy of all acceptation, that Christ Jesus came into the world to save sinners; of whom I am chief.* God in the flesh came to earth, lived a sinless life, and then gave His life on a cruel cross. When He shed His blood and died, it was to pay the price for our sin. He did it so that we could be cleared from our sin-debt, be forgiven, and have eternal life!" Mark flipped over to the book of Ephesians in his Bible and pointed to verse seven. "Read this good news here."

"In whom we have redemption through his blood, the forgiveness of sins, according to the riches of his grace;" Jessa read out loud.

"And you know what happened three days after His crucifixion . . . ."

"He rose from the dead."

"Exactly! He was completely victorious over sin and death, defeating Satan, and offering us salvation. Romans 6:23 says, *For the wages of sin is death; but the gift of God is eternal life through Jesus Christ our Lord.* Now, here's an amazing thing about God. He doesn't force anyone to take this gift of eternal life, even though He already paid for it. He offers it to each person, but it is not theirs unless they accept the gift." Mark wanted to share a verse about this, but his mind suddenly went completely blank. He flipped to the front of his Bible where he had left a gospel tract. It was filled with good salvation verses. As his eyes skimmed the back page, he spotted a good verse to use. "Romans 4:5 says, *But to him that worketh not, but believeth on him that justifieth the ungodly, his faith is counted for righteousness.* According to this verse, our eternal salvation is not based upon our works. We are saved the moment we put our faith in God, trusting in what Jesus did for us on the cross." He paused, trying to interpret Jessa's expression.

"Jessa, have you ever made the decision to trust the Lord as your personal Savior?"

Her eyes once again were welling up with tears. "I can't say I have. I've heard most of this before, but you explained it much more clearly. I've always viewed what I knew about the Bible as 'religion' . . . like . . . not really personal, you know? But Jesus really gives us each a chance to personally accept what He's done, doesn't He?"

"He does. And even more than that, he gives us the opportunity to know and enjoy Him personally every day for the rest of our lives!"

"Mark, with every part of my being I want to be saved! I understand things better now, and I trust Jesus Christ as my Savior. This is real! Like . . . I believe He died and rose again for *me personally!* I've just never seen it this way before!"

Mark beamed, as he turned to another Bible passage. "I am rejoicing with you, Sister! Look at what it says here in Ephesians one. *In whom ye also trusted, after that ye heard the word of truth, the gospel of your salvation: in whom also after that ye believed, ye were sealed with that holy Spirit of promise, ...* Now that you've believed the gospel, you are completely forgiven of all sin, forever! Romans 5:1 says, *Therefore being justified by faith, we have peace with God through our Lord Jesus Christ:*"

Jessa scooted herself up in the hospital bed, tears now freely trickling down her face. "God sent you here, Mark. He knew I was looking for answers. You don't know how scared I've been since the accident . . . wondering what would have happened to me if I had died." She paused for a moment and then added, "Now I know where I would have gone – hell. Thank God for saving my life in the accident and giving me another chance to accept the gospel!"

"Yes, praise the Lord! Let's stop right now and thank Him for all that He's done."

The two bowed their heads and each expressed their hearts of gratitude to God.

Later, as Mark prepared to leave, he scribbled a Bible reference on a piece of paper and then added his phone number on the reverse side. Handing it to Jessa, he said, "Think about what Christ has done for you, and then read this verse. I'll be praying for you as my new sister in Christ. You are welcome to call me if you need to."

Almost before he had entered the hall, Jessa reached for the Bible her dad had left on the nightstand, and found the verse Mark had referenced. Colossians 3:13. The message of the verse was a clear and convicting one: *Forbearing one another, and forgiving one another, if any man have a quarrel against any: even as Christ forgave you, so also do ye.*

Charlie Kallenbach opened the front door with enthusiastic expectancy. Coming up the sidewalk was a brother in the Lord whom he was excited to see. Mark's genuine change of heart had been evident in the email he had sent to Charlie just two days prior. After visiting Jessa in the hospital, Mark sent a last minute text to see if Charlie and Sarah were open to a visit. They lived just 30 minutes off his route in Alabama.

"Come on in, Brother!" he said after giving him a hearty handshake and pat on the shoulder. "We're so glad you decided to stop by!" Something about Charlie's mannerisms reminded Mark so much of Hannah. This was, after all, her older brother. And his laugh . . . it was just like hers.

Charlie had a very bold way about him. Usually it served him well, but he had to guard himself from being too impulsive or overbearing. His wife, Sarah, was a sweet, quiet woman who admired her husband's courage to stand up and proclaim the truth in every situation. She was glad to see the godly influence he had had on Mark in the recent years since they met him and his sister, Grace.

As Charlie and Sarah conversed with Mark about the events of the past summer, and all that God had done in Mark's life, an idea started rolling around in Charlie's mind.

Pressing Toward the Mark

"Mark, I've got a good friend who's a pilot. His name is Pete; he's a few years older than myself. He's ferrying a plane down to Colombia for a mission organization there. He'll be flying the plane full of Bibles and other materials for the missionaries and then catching a commercial flight back home. I think you should go with him."

"Okay, why?" The look on Mark's face was a mixture of intrigue and uncertainty.

"I just think it might be a good experience for you. With all that you've been through lately, I think it would do you good, and it would bless Pete to have a guy to go with him."

Mark's mind ran back to that day when Jerome had convinced him to get his passport just in case a travelling opportunity came up. Mark leaned forward, leaning his elbows on his knees with his hands folded. "When is your friend going?"

"I don't know. Sometime soon. He might have gone already, but I don't think so. I'll call him tonight if you want me to and talk to him about it."

"Okay. I'm open to the idea of going, but I don't want to commit until I know more."

"Actually, why don't I call him right now," Charlie said picking up his phone. This guy knew how to get things done. After selecting Pete from his contacts, he hit the call button and then put it on speaker phone.

"Hey, Charlie!" Pete's voice sounded on the other end.

"Hi Pete! Are you still stateside?"

"Yes, Sir. Why?"

"Do you remember what Psalm 37:37 says?"

"Um . . . Is this a serious question, or . . . ?"

Charlie chuckled with a mischievous grin. "It says 'Mark the perfect man' and I think I have the 'perfect' man to go with you to Colombia. His name is even Mark!"

The smile on Pete's face could be heard in his voice. "I think that's applying the verse a little differently than it was meant to be. But do you really have a friend who'd want to go along?"

Charlie looked questioningly at Mark. "Not quite sure yet, but I think so. He's visiting us today. I've got you on speaker phone so he and my wife can hear. When are you flying out?"

"In three days. I'm leaving on Saturday."

Sarah, who was trying to keep her one-year-old entertained and quiet, mouthed to her husband, "How long will he be in Colombia?"

"Did you say you'd be gone for a week?" Charlie asked Pete.

"Yes, but it may end up being more like ten days depending on how much is going on there, and what we can help the missionaries with. I'd love to have a brother in the Lord to make the trip with me and help when we're down there. I've got a couple thousand Spanish Bibles ready to be loaded into the plane. Help with that alone would be huge."

Several thoughts presented themselves in Mark's mind. Perhaps this is what Hannah wanted him to do . . . going on a mission trip. Maybe things between them could work out. But would that be his motivation for going? It didn't seem like a good reason. Besides, Hannah had that handsome, cool-truck-driving Jasper now, so it wouldn't make a difference anyway. Regardless of all that, the trip did sound like a neat opportunity to help spread the gospel and encourage missionaries. He had less than three days to make a decision. Maybe Jerome's idea of rock climbing in Greece hadn't been God's will, but what about mission work in Colombia?

Mark's attention was drawn to the phone conversation again when Pete addressed him directly. "Mark, any friend of Charlie's is a friend of mine. And if he recommends you, I'd be very happy to have you go with me."

"Thanks," Mark responded, not sure what to say. "Can I think and pray about it and let you know tomorrow?"

"Definitely."

Back in Indiana, the next morning dawned with magnificent rays of sun piercing through the thick fog. The dew lay heavily on the Kallenbach farm. The third week of August was one the family looked forward to all year. It had become an annual ministry to travel to the State Fair and facilitate a gospel booth.

Everyone awoke early to load the 15-passenger van and head out for the long road trip. Grace and Zack were excited to be a part of it this year and arrived at the Kallenbachs early enough to help with packing all the last minute things. Finally, an hour and fifteen minutes later than the planned departure time, the Kallenbachs, Grace, Zack, and two other friends piled into the van and headed out of the driveway. Road trips with a big family were always interesting. Grace had to smile when Joey and nine-year-old Tyler, each brought a dangerous bowl of spillable cereal and milk to eat on the way.

Joey was the first to say something about it. "Tyler, you better not spill that on me! I only brought one pair of pants."

"What? I brought six!"

"Why? We're only going to be gone for five days!"

"Yeah, but if the van breaks down and I want to help Daniel fix it, I'll want a pair of pants I can get dirty." At that moment, the van drove over some railroad tracks, jostling the threatening bowls of cereal and milk. "Watch out, Joey! You almost spilled milk all over me! I should have worn my dirty pants and changed when we got there."

Grace shook her head smiling. Those boys were something else.

After an hour on the road, everyone had settled down and found something to do. Some of them were sleeping, some were reading a book, some were playing the Alphabet Game, and the younger kids were coloring in their special "travel coloring books." Grace was contentedly gazing out the window when loud exotic jungle noises jolted her from her thoughts. "Huh? Oh yeah, that's my phone!" She laughed as she picked it up.

"Hi Mark! Your mischievous habit of changing ringtones is contagious," she said with playfulness in her voice.

"Oh yeah? Who's ringtone did you change?"

"My own! And I almost didn't recognize my phone was ringing just now because of it."

Mark chuckled. "Well, other than that, how is your day going?"

Hannah, who was sitting in the seat next to Grace, listened to Grace's side of the conversation with utmost interest. Grace told Mark about their plans for the weekend, and the interesting start to the morning. After being filled in, Mark broached her with the question on his mind: What did she think about the Colombia opportunity?

"I think I should just do it," he said after talking through it with her. "I've prayed about it, and I don't see any reason I shouldn't go. And I see a lot of good reasons for going. But what are your thoughts?"

"It really sounds like a good opportunity, if you ask me. I'm a little surprised to hear you're considering it though. You've never talked about taking a mission trip before."

Hannah lifted one eyebrow, wondering what all this was about.

"I know. God has used the events of this past year to show me some things . . . and this trip just seems to be the right thing, at the right time."

"Then go for it." Grace smiled confidently as she turned and looked at Hannah. "I've got to go, Mark. Looks like we're stopping for a bathroom break. Please be praying for our outreach this week, and let me know what you decide about Colombia."

"I'm deciding right now, to go, Grace. I'd appreciate your prayers as well."

"Great! I'm excited for you! I'll definitely be praying. Hey, why don't we talk again before you fly out?"

"Sure. I'll try to call Saturday morning."

"Sounds good. Hasta luego, Hermano!"

"Hasta luego."

Chapter Nine

*M*ark sat down with Charlie and Sarah in their living room one last time before leaving for the airport. Sarah was glad the baby was still sleeping quietly and wouldn't be a distraction. The three bowed their heads and prayed together. The way Charlie talked with the Lord was so genuine and deep. Mark wanted to be a man of prayer like that.

"Lord God, You are the one who created us and put us on this earth for a purpose. You saved us and called us with a holy calling. Thank You, Father . . . ." Charlie paused as a joyful smile spread across his face. "Thank You so much . . . . It's our desire to live lives that please and glorify You. Thank You for this opportunity You've given Mark to see another part of Your creation, and minister to people of another culture. We ask for Your love and power to go with him and flow through him to others. Teach him, Lord, whatever You want him to learn through this. Please protect him, both spiritually and physically. Your will be done.

"We also pray for the rest of my family and Grace and Zack as they share the gospel at the fair. Bless them and lead them to the right people. Help the seed of truth that they are sowing to fall on good soil. Lord Jesus, there are still so many souls heading straight for hell. Open their eyes, God, that they may see their sin and the horror of its end. Lead those lost and wandering souls to Your cross! And help us to be faithful witnesses for You. As Charles Spurgeon said, 'If sinners will be damned, at least let them leap to hell over our bodies. And if they will perish, let them perish with our arms around their knees, imploring them to stay. If hell must be filled, at least let it be filled in the teeth of our exertions, and let not one go there unwarned and unprayed for.' Lord, I know You are doing great things that are sometimes unseen to man. I praise You for your wondrous works! I know there are people at the fair today that are open to the gospel. For their sake, I pray for them to have no peace or even sleep until they turn to you as their all-sufficient Savior! I pray this in the Name above all names, Jesus. Amen."

"Amen," Mark and Sarah echoed.

Charlie looked at the time on his phone. "Okay, Mark, I should get you over to the airport. Pete will need our help loading all those Bibles."

"Right," Mark agreed, standing up and swinging his backpack over his shoulder.

The two men drove about 20 minutes to the small airport where Pete and the Cessna 402 mission plane were waiting.

As they pulled into the parking lot, Mark wrestled with second thoughts. Was he really going to get on a plane headed for a foreign country, with a man he had never even met? But Pete was a friend of Charlie, and a brother in the Lord. At this point, there was no turning back for Mark. He would trust God and go.

Grace grabbed another stack of tracts from Zack's backpack. The two of them had found a good place right outside of the fairgrounds where they could hand out tracts to people coming and going. Inside of the grounds, several members of the Kallenbach family manned a booth where they offered free tracts, Bibles, and other Christian materials to people. They took "shifts" throughout the week so that everyone had something to help with and also had time to pray and rest.

Grace reminisced about the first time she and her brother had gone witnessing with the Kallenbachs, less than three years ago. She remembered the very real discouragement and lies the Devil threw her way leading up to the event. Yes, when a Christian sets out to do God's will, it is more than likely he will face spiritual opposition. The Devil is utterly threatened by saints who are willing soldiers of Christ, armed with the armor of God. How wonderfully God had blessed her that day at the festival. He led her to Jackie, a young girl who was hungry for truth. The joy Grace experienced seeing Jackie trust Jesus as her Savior was worth the battle she had faced to be there. Oh, it was such an honor to lead a soul to Christ!

Pressing Toward the Mark

Grace's thoughts were brought back to the present when she noticed a young man in his twenties walking directly toward her and Zack. He looked like he was on a mission. His girlfriend followed close behind him. "Can I have one of what you're handing out?" he asked, referring to the gospel tracts. "What organization are you guys with?"

Zack readily gave them both a tract and then began to explain. "We are not part of any organization. We are just Christians who love to share the good news of Jesus Christ with the world!"

"So you don't have to do this? Like, no one makes you come out here?"

"No, definitely not." Zack and Grace both confirmed.

Grace clarified further, saying, "The love that God has put in our hearts for people is what motivates us to be out here."

"Okay. I was just wondering," the young man went on, "because I came out of a background where we had to record our hours of door-knocking outreach. I always felt bound by it... like if I didn't do enough I might not have eternal life in the Kingdom."

"Jehovah's Witness?" Zack surmised.

"Yeah, you guessed! But not any more!" He motioned his hand dismissively.

"So you left the Watch Tower Society? Tell me more about why you left."

"Well, it was a bunch of little things that added up. One thing that bothered me was the ultimate authority they give to the Watch Tower Society. I mean, it's like, whatever they say is from God and you better obey it!"

"So do you believe we have access to any true words from God today?" Before going any further Zack wanted to establish the Bible as God's authoritative, pure Word.

"Only the Bible I guess . . . but even that has been changed and messed with."

"You bring up an interesting point. I agree with you that the Bible is the only Word of God. As far as it being changed and messed with, that's true of many of the English Bible versions. But the amazing thing is that God has kept one Bible pure and preserved for us!"

Now the young man's girlfriend began to participate in the conversation. "I'd love to know which Bible THAT is," she said with a little exasperation.

Zack continued to explain. "Well, the history of the Bible is fascinating. Did you know that throughout the centuries there have been two distinct versions, or lines, of 'original language' manuscripts?"

"What do you mean?" She looked confused.

"There are the manuscripts referred to as the Traditional Text that was used by the early church. It has been trusted, used and translated for centuries by God's people. And the *other* line of manuscripts is called the Modern Text. These manuscripts differ from the Traditional Text, *and* from each other. "

"Interesting, I never knew that!" The couple was surprised. The young man had more questions as he processed what

Zack had just said. "But even though some of the words are translated a little differently from one Bible version to another, don't they all get the same message across?"

"That's what a lot of people like to believe. But the truth is, every word is significant and has a unique meaning. Even the tiniest difference in a word or punctuation can change important doctrine. Many of the modern Bible versions omit crucial words, phrases and sometimes entire verses. Important words like Christ, Lord, and Son of God are removed, as well as words that point to the deity of Christ and his shed blood!"

"Wow," the girlfriend interjected. "So how about the JW's Bible, the New World Translation? Which text was that translated from?"

"Well, believe it or not," Zack said adjusting the weight of the backpack on his shoulders, "almost all modern English Bible versions are translated from the Modern Text, while the King James Version uses the Traditional Text. The New World Translation uses the 1881 Wescott-Hort text which goes back to the corrupt Modern Text."

"Huh."

"People have come up to me before accusing God's Word of having errors in it. They take me to verses like 2 Samuel 21:19, which in many Bibles states that Elhanan killed Goliath."

"Really? Everybody knows David killed Goliath," the couple reasoned. "So what's the answer?"

"When they say the Bible has errors," Zack said sliding the backpack off his shoulders and pulling out his Bible, "I show them 2 Samuel 21:19 in the King James Bible." He flipped the pages to the passage and pointed out verse. "Notice that here in the King James Bible it says that Elhanan killed *the brother of* Goliath."

"Wow, that's major!" The young man said emphatically. "You know, I think I need to go buy myself a King James Bible!"

Zack and Grace smiled. It was so refreshing to talk to someone with an open heart, ready to learn and hear truth.

Grace wanted to circle around again to the gospel. "So you came out of the Jehovah's Witness movement," she said addressing the man, and then turned to his girlfriend, "and how about you? Do you have any religious background?"

"Yeah, when I was little my mom took me to church, but I never really got into it myself." She seemed a little fidgety, and paused for a moment before saying more. "Okay, so here's *my* hang-up," she said abruptly. "I'm not trying to step on any toes or anything, but from what I've seen, pretty much all religions have the same ideas and rules. They just label them a little differently. It's basically like, do your best to live a good moral life to stay on good terms with your God, and hopefully you'll make it to a good place after you die."

"You've hit on a very important point," Grace responded. "All religions, except one, teach that you must do things for God to have eternal life. But Christianity stands apart because it teaches that God has done the work for us to to have eternal life."

"But when I was growing up, they taught us in the church that if we weren't baptized and living a holy life we would not go to heaven. And if we didn't forgive others, God wouldn't forgive us!"

"Well, there's one big reason a lot of people get confused and start teaching a mixed message," Zack explained. "When we read the Bible, it's crucial that we pay attention to the context of what we're reading and who it was originally written to. If we don't, we can get into trouble."

"Like . . . give me an example." The young lady seemed genuinely hungry to understand.

"Well, here's an obvious one, but it makes my point. If you flip your Bible open to Genesis 6:14 and start reading, you will see that it commands to build an ark. We all know that God is not commanding us to build an ark today. That command was given specifically to Noah for a specific time and purpose. Now, with that in mind, let's consider the New Testament. In the Gospels Jesus does not die on the cross until the very end of the books. During His whole time on earth ministering in human flesh, Jesus was preaching the law and the prophets. He was the prophesied Messiah of Israel and was about to set up His Kingdom right there in Jerusalem. He said the Kingdom of Heaven was at hand."

"So, what you're implying . . . " the young man deduced, "is that we should look at what Jesus taught like we look at the Old Testament?"

"Right. In Matthew 15:24 Jesus said, *I am not sent but unto the lost sheep of the house of Israel.* Just like we read, study, and apply lessons from the Old Testament, we cherish the Scriptures about the life of Jesus. But the preaching of the law and the earthly Kingdom in the Gospels is much different from the message the Apostle Paul preached later on."

"Right." Grace commented. "Going back to what you said earlier," she said addressing the girlfriend, "about forgiving others to be forgiven by God, I just looked up a verse about that." She held her Bible so the couple could read along. "Mark 11:26 *But if ye do not forgive, neither will your Father which is in heaven forgive your trespasses.* But now read what God had Paul write in Ephesians." She turned the pages over to Ephesians 4:32 and read aloud. *"And be ye kind one to another, tenderhearted, forgiving one another, even as God for Christ's sake hath forgiven you."*

The young lady paused thoughtfully for a moment. "So one verse is saying forgive to be forgiven, and the other is saying forgive because you have been forgiven?"

"Exactly. And the reason is that in Mark, we are reading the teachings under the law. In Ephesians we are reading the teachings under grace."

"Yeah," Zack affirmed. "After God saved the Apostle Paul, He revealed something to him that was kept secret up until that point. Paul called it 'the mystery'. He explains about it in Ephesians chapter three. What Israel didn't know through prophesy was that there would be an interruption in the story of God's workings with Israel, and, like Ephesians 3:6 says, *That the Gentiles should be fellowheirs, and of the same body, and partakers of his promise in Christ by the gospel:* Before God revealed this to Paul, there was a big difference between the Jews and everyone else. If you wanted to have eternal life, you had to access God through the Jews and the Law of Moses."

"But now we can all come through Jesus," the young man concluded for him.

"Right! Romans chapter three lays it all out clearly. First it explains that the law was given to show us that we could never keep God's law, we have all sinned and we need a Savior." Zack flipped the pages of his Bible to Romans chapter three. "Read what it says here," he said pointing to verses 21-23."

The man read slowly and thoughtfully. *"But now the righteousness of God without the law is manifested, being witnessed by the law and the prophets; Even the righteousness of God which is by faith of Jesus Christ unto all and upon all them that believe: for there is no difference: For all have sinned, and come short of the glory of God;"*

"Great. Now read verse 28."

"Therefore we conclude that a man is justified by faith without the deeds of the law."

"So according to this verse, we are saved by faith plus what?"

"Nothing," the two listeners responded in unison.

"Uh huh. And in chapter five he confirms this again, saying, 'Therefore being justified by faith, we have peace with God through our Lord Jesus Christ:'"

"Man, nobody has ever explained it to me that way before," the young man said gratefully.

"Me either," his girlfriend agreed. "I need to go home and think about this more."

"They've already got me convinced," the young man said energetically. "It feels so freeing to take the pressure of always trying to measure up off my back. According to those verses you showed us, what Jesus did on my behalf was enough to save me."

Zack smiled. "That's right!

"So . . . that's it then?" The young man squinted in the blinding summer sun. "Am I supposed to like, go to church and walk down the aisle or something?"

"No, that's not necessary. Salvation is a transaction between you and God. He offers you salvation as a free gift, and you receive it by faith. If you believe the gospel, which we've just explained, then why don't you pray right now and tell God that you trust in Him to save you. Thank Him for His forgiveness."

The young man had no reservations about doing this in the middle of the bustle of fair-goers. He bowed his head and with a few simple, heartfelt sentences, asked God to save him.

When he had concluded, Zack gave him a joyful hug, and Grace blinked away thankful tears. The girlfriend looked both intrigued, and happy for him at the same time.

Zack put a hand on the young man's shoulder. "Now that you have received salvation from God, what do you think your life should be about?"

"Well, about Him, I guess!"

"Read Ephesians 2:8-10 when you get home as a reminder."

"Oh yeah, I will. And after that, where should I read?"

"Start with the epistles of Paul - Romans through Philemon. That's where you'll find direct instructions for us in this period of God's plan. And don't forget," Zack added, "all of the Bible is profitable for us!"

The young man left Zack with his phone number so they could talk again. After saying goodbye, the two disappeared again into the massive crowd.

"And we're off again," Pete said as the wheels of the Cessna left the runway. He made it look so easy. Mark wondered how long Pete had been flying planes. Mark was finally beginning to enjoy take off and landing. A few stops for fuel along the way had cured him of his uneasy nerves.

"So what got you interested in flying, Pete?" he asked as the plane rapidly gained altitude, gently pressing the men into their seats.

"Oh, I've always been fascinated by planes and aviation. I can remember, even as a little boy, when we would drop my dad off at the airport for a business trip, my mom would practically have to drag me back to the car. I wanted to stay all day and watch the planes come and go."

"How did you get involved in aviation?"

"When I was seventeen I started flying lessons, and I loved it. I wasn't sure what I wanted to do with the skill, other than using it for fun. There was, of course, the option of getting a commercial pilot's license and flying big planes for the airlines . . . and there was the option of flying in the U.S. Air Force. While I was trying to figure all of that out, a pretty girl became part of my life and all of my decisions seemed to be impacted by that relationship. She meant the world to me and I wanted to marry her."

Mark gazed out the window at the distant earth beneath. He could relate. Hannah meant the world to him. Somehow, though, the lofty view from the plane gliding through the clear air gave him a sense of stepping back and seeing the big picture of life. How incredible that the Creator sees the entire picture, and all of the universe, yet cares about the very tiny details of our lives!

"Just when I was planning a romantic proposal, I found out she was going on dates with my best friend from high school. When I confronted her she said she only planned to date us both until she could decide between us. And that day, it was clear she was choosing my friend over me. I was devastated."

At least Hannah had a good reason for not marrying me. She would never do what Pete's girlfriend did. Mark's heart throbbed a little harder as he thought about the purity and virtue of the woman he loved.

Pete leveled off from the climb, reduced power to the engines, and adjusted the trim. He then continued his story. "I did what so many young men do when they want to run away from their problems. I joined the military. I was encouraged to fly in the Air Force, and they told me thrilling stories about being a fighter jet pilot." Pete chuckled. "They couldn't convince me though. I was willing to fight in the war, but I didn't want to couple fighting and killing with the thing I loved to do – flying. I knew flying would never be the same for me if I joined the Air force. So . . . I chose the Army."

"Did things get better after you joined the military or did the problem just get worse?" Mark asked. He had run away from his problems too, but they had continued to stare him in the face until he dealt with them.

"No, Mark. I went into the military with a broken heart. And I didn't want to face the reality of the rejection from my girlfriend. Basic training required all my focus and energy, so sometimes I would forget about my pain. But at night as I lay in my bunk, I couldn't get away from my misery. I wasn't a believer at the time, so I had no answers. I didn't like to talk about it with anybody, but one of my buddies pried it out of me. Once he heard my story, he suggested I talk to the Chaplain. God used that Chaplain to show me my sinful state before a holy God. He explained to me how Jesus came to die in my place and give me eternal life if I would only trust Him as my Savior. I became a Christian that day, and though there were still many rough roads ahead, God was there to walk them with me.

"By the end of my four-year term with the military, I was a different man. I was determined to face life's problems by God's grace, rather than run away from them. I resumed my flight training and went on to become a commercial airline pilot. That's what I do now for a living. With my vacation time I love flying for missionaries, helping to bring supplies to and from wherever needed. I got connected to Ed Winston and the mission down there in Colombia about three years ago. And the rest is history, I guess."

"Wow! You have a neat story. Thanks for sharing it with me," Mark responded. He glanced down at Pete's left hand. No ring. "I take it you're still single?"

"Right. I haven't found the right woman yet.... I sometimes wonder if marriage isn't part of God's plan for me. And if so, I'm totally content with that. I am able to serve Him in ways that I couldn't if I had a wife and kids. I'm learning, Mark, that the most important mission in life is to bring souls to Christ... no matter who or where they are. For some people, that might mean teaching their own children the gospel, and for others, like myself right now, it means witnessing to coworkers, and making trips to Colombia."

Mark smiled. *Thank you, Lord, for introducing me to this brother. You knew I could relate to his story. Thanks for allowing me to take this trip with him.*

It was a rainy day in Alabama. Gentle thunder rumbled in the clouds above. Mr. Keller pulled into an empty spot in the hospital's parking ramp. He was relieved that he wouldn't have to walk through the rain. His wife sat in the passenger seat. They had sat in silence the last 15 minutes of their drive. As they unbuckled their seat belts, Mrs. Keller spoke. "Richard, do you think she's going to be okay now?"

"They did say she's well enough to be released today," he said, straightening his collar.

"I mean her heart. Last time you saw her she was so angry she wouldn't let you stay."

"I know. But now she requested we both come get her and bring her home. I think she'll be alright."

"What do you think she needs to talk to us about? She sounded pretty serious when she mentioned it on the phone . . . ."

"I don't know, Marge. But I'm slowly coming to realize that things are not really in our hands. It's taken a lot for me to admit it, but . . . I think we just have to trust God to make things okay between us and our daughter again. Come on, let's go in and see her."

The two made their way into the hospital, and after stopping at the front desk, identified the correct floor and room where Jessa could be found. As they neared her room, a knot began to form in Mr. Keller's stomach. Just then, from behind them a very familiar voice called, "Mom! Dad!" They turned to see Jessa coming toward them on crutches.

In a moment the three were united with a series of hugs and tears, with crutches awkwardly getting in the way.

"I am so glad to see both of you," Jessa said, wiping tears from her cheeks. "And I am so ready to go home!"

"We've missed you so much, Honey," her mother said brushing Jessa's hair away from her face. Mr. Keller nodded in agreement.

"Let's go down the hall and sit down," Jessa suggested. "There's a nice lobby area down there where we can talk."

After they each found a comfortable place to sit, Jessa addressed her father. "Dad, last time you were here, you asked me to forgive you . . . and I wasn't willing to. I felt like you didn't have a clue how much you were asking me to forgive you for. I was wrong in the way I responded to you. Now I need to ask you to forgive *me* for being angry with you."

"You don't need to apologize, Jessa," Mr. Keller interjected. His next words were ones Jessa wondered if she had ever heard him say before. "I was very wrong." He looked away down the hall, swallowing away his pride and the tears that threatened to show themselves. Jessa tried to process the humble change in her father. Saying "sorry" or "forgive me" was one thing, but clearly admitting he was wrong was another. He turned his head and looked her in the eye. "I don't blame you for being angry with me."

"I know, Dad, but I want you to know that I forgive you. And I am sorry for being angry. God has shown me my own sin, and He has forgiven me completely, even though it cost Him everything. After all that He has done for me, how can I refuse to forgive others? All my life, I had the idea that I was going to heaven because I was raised in a Christian family. But after my accident, God showed me that I was not saved. I've decided to trust Him personally as my Savior. Christianity is so real to me now. It's not just a name."

"That's really good to hear, Jessa," her father said, tears welling up in his eyes again. He was determined not to let them overflow; he never cried in front of anyone. In the past few weeks the term "Christian" had taken on a much deeper meaning for him too, even though he had been saved for years.

Pressing Toward the Mark

Mrs. Keller put her arm around Jessa's shoulder. "We love you, Honey. Why don't we go home and start fresh?"

"Yes, I'm ready. But can we stop one place before we head home?"

"Where's that?"

"Mamaw's. I know we'd be backtracking to get there, but I'd really like to talk to her about all that's happened."

Her parents nodded in unison. "Absolutely. She and Papaw will be delighted to see all of us."

Chapter Ten

"You are a God-send, Pete," the mission director said as they finished securing the airplane in the mission hangar. "When we built this hangar and landing strip four years ago the mission didn't own a plane, but we've been praying that God would provide one. It's been amazing to watch how He opened the doors for the mission to buy this one. It's a gift from God, and we are so grateful to you for delivering it to us!"

Pete gave the plane a satisfied pat, "It's my pleasure, Sir. I'm thankful we got her here safe and sound."

"We?" Mark laughed.

"Well, I'd say you make a pretty good co-pilot for never having flown before," Pete joked. "Even if you don't know much about flying, I think we make for pretty good travel companions!"

"We're glad to have both of you here for a few days. Ed and Erica Winston are coming to pick you up and should be here any minute."

The three men made their way out of the hangar and toward the mission headquarters. Mark loved the look of the rich green foliage along the pathway. Plantain trees with their huge thick leaves waved in the wind, and growing beneath them were shorter plants with beautiful red flowers.

The director continued. "I think the Winstons have a lot planned for the next week and they're hoping you will participate."

Mark and Pete responded affirmatively.

"Will we have a chance to meet your regular mission pilot while we're here?" Pete inquired.

"No, unfortunately not. He's doing a survey trip up north right now, and won't be back for a few weeks."

"How far from here do the Winstons live?" Mark asked.

"Oh, they're about 45 minutes from here."

Pete explained their location more fully. "So right now we are pretty close to Palmira, about an hour east of Cali. We're in what's called the Valle del Cauca department of Colombia. The Winstons live in the same department, but a little ways northwest."

As Pete was finishing his sentence, a man and woman came excitedly toward them. "Pete, you made it!"

"Yes, Sir, we did!" Pete exchanged hand shakes with the couple and then introduced Mark to their missionary hosts.

"Yo tengo gozo, gozo, en mi corazón!" The joyful chorus emanated from the exuberant group gathered around the fire. The tune was a familiar one to Mark, and he remembered singing it at Bible camp as a kid. *I have the joy, joy, joy, joy, down in my heart.* It almost didn't seem real that he was here in South America . . . breathing in the humid jungle air . . . and hearing the sound of countless birds and insects, melding their authentic song with the "gozo, gozo" of these village people. The Winston family lived at the edge of a little "pueblo," or town, at the foot of the mountains. The beauty of this land was breath-taking. Mark enjoyed the natural wonders back home, like the Rockies and the Grand Canyon, but the magnificent, untamed mountains of Colombia had a special appeal to him. *Lord, You are an amazing Creator,* he had prayed on the drive from the mission headquarters to the Winstons' home.

It was the third day since they had arrived. From the moment they landed, there had not been a quiet moment. Ed and his family lead many ongoing ministries in the pueblo, as well as efforts to reach out to the mountain folk. In anticipation of Pete's visit, and the Bibles he would be bringing, they planned extra outreaches for the week. Tonight, they had invited the public for a time of singing, testimonies, and food in their backyard. Ed's oldest daughter also did a chalk drawing of a cross, bridging the gap between man and God. She drew this visual of the gospel, while her father explained the plan of salvation. As the night drew on, and songs filled the air, Mark sat back and observed the people... the faces... the clothes.... There was so much happiness. These people didn't have much in terms of everyday things, but did that matter to them? It didn't seem to keep them from having a good time. The carefree, happy demeanor of these simple people reminded him of little children. Lack of money and technology can have some benefits... contrary to the modern American ideology.

A young boy, about the age of 12, caught Mark's eye. While everyone else around the fire seemed to have forgotten their problems, this boy's face said something different. Mark watched as he quietly stood up and slipped away from the light of the fire. Mark's eyes tried to adjust as he squinted after him into the darkness. A gunnysack? How did that fit in the boy's pocket? Now he was squatting down and picking something up from the ground. He was collecting something and quickly stashing it away in his sack. Mark looked up at the tree looming overhead, then back at the fruit on the ground. Mangos?

Just then, Ed walked by and saw Mark looking toward the mango tree. "Ah...." he said nodding in the boy's direction. "That's Manuel. A few days after the mangos started falling from our tree, I found him in our back yard filling his gunnysack as fast as he could. Someone told him we were gone that day so he found a way to climb the wall that surrounds our property and started loading up with our mangos."

"What did you do when you caught him?"

Pressing Toward the Mark

"I stood and watched him for a few minutes before approaching him. That gave me a moment to think and ask God what I should do. As I stood there, God gave me compassion for the boy, instead of anger. I walked up and greeted him like a friend. He was so scared that he grabbed his sack and tried to make it over the wall but fell backwards onto the ground. I leaned over him and held out a hand to help him up. 'Son, don't worry,' I said in Spanish. 'If you need mangos, just ask me. We have enough to share.' He looked at me in disbelief and didn't say a word. Then I explained to him how stealing is wrong, and by taking the mangos without asking, he was stealing from me. I made a deal with him. First, I told him that he could not have any stolen mangos – so I took back all the mangos he had in his sack. Then I told him he could have any of the remaining mangos on the ground as a gift. He didn't believe me at first, but after saying it three times, he thanked me with tears in his eyes. He gathered every last one of the good mangos from the ground. 'I tell you what,' I said to him, 'if you agree to not steal from anyone, then you can come back as many times as you want and get mangos.' He was so excited! I later learned that he lives with his mother and three siblings. His father left them, and the family has very little food or money. Manuel does what he can to find food . . . even if it means stealing. He still feels uncomfortable about taking my mangos, so he usually comes after dark."

By now, Manuel's sack was nearly full of fruit. He worked fast. "I wish I knew Spanish well enough to talk to him," Mark commented.

"Well, do you know enough to introduce yourself?" Ed asked.

Pressing Toward the Mark

"Me llamo Mark. ¿Como se llama?"

"There you go! You can try it and see what happens."

Manuel was now filling a second sack. Mark slipped away from the circle and walked over to the mango tree. "Buenas noches. Me llamo Mark. ¿Como se llama?"

The boy paused and looked up startled. "Manuel," was the one word response. *Okay, that was a pretty good start, but now what do I say?* The boy mumbled something in Spanish, and then continued gathering mangos. "I can help you," Mark said smiling. The two worked in awkward silence, each thinking thoughts about the other in their own language. Mark hoped that even without words, Manuel would know that he cared.

The drive from Mamaw's house back to California was no small distance. It did, however, provide Jessa and her parents many hours to talk.

"But why Georgia?" her mother questioned. "We don't know anyone there, other than your grandmother. What would cause you to go there?"

"I wanted to visit the town where Jerome grew up and went to college," Jessa explained.

Her dad didn't make the connection. "But if Jerome wasn't there, why would you want to go?"

"Dad, I wanted to prove to you that Jerome was not a looser. He had a good heart!"

Silence claimed the small space in the car for a moment, as Mr. Keller once again regretted the moves he had made.

Jessa let out a sigh and then continued. "I found out a lot about Jerome while I was there. I made a lot of connections and talked to people he grew up with and went to school with. They told me what they knew about him, but none of it was surprising. They knew the same adventure-loving Jerome that I did."

"So were you satisfied with your efforts?" her mother asked.

"Not until I talked with those who knew him when he was in college."

"I thought he didn't go to college," Mr. Keller interrupted.

"He did go, but never finished." She had the full attention of both her parents now. With emotions of fresh pain overlayed with forgiveness, Jessa went on to tell the rest of Jerome's story.

After she had explained Jerome's reason for leaving Georgia, Mr. Keller summed up the story. "So he left town and went to California, where he met a girl with a thirst for adventure like himself...." A sense of remorse floated on his words. "And then her heartless old father . . ."

Jessa cut him off before he could finish. "Dad, that's all said and dealt with now. We don't have to go over that again."

"I know, Jessa, but I feel so awful now about what I did. Not only did I reject him as a looser, but then I had to go write a stupid forged text just days before the guy was on his deathbed!" Mr. Keller rubbed his forehead with his fingers.

"Dad. *I forgive you.*" She paused a moment and looked out the car window. Then turning to him again, she said softly, "Can you forgive yourself?"

His wife watched him to see his response.

"Yes." He said this word with humble determination. "I know I've got to, or my life will become even more of a mess. I know that God, and you, have forgiven me, so I'm willing to forgive myself too."

"I have to confess, though," Jessa said soberly, "that I didn't use much discernment concerning my relationship with Jerome. I wasn't interested in learning about his spiritual and moral convictions. I guess it's because I wasn't sure about my own convictions. As my father, you had a right to tell me not to date an unbeliever . . . . But I don't think that was the reason you forbade me from seeing him . . . but anyway . . . ."

"I wasn't being a loving protector for you as I should have been. I was doing things for all the wrong reasons. Can you forgive me for this too?"

"Yes! Let's start over, okay?"

"It's a deal."

Mrs. Keller reached over and gave her husband a loving squeeze on the arm. With God as the center of their family, she knew things were headed in the right direction.

It was early Wednesday morning in Colombia. Mark awoke to the distinct chirps of loud birds outside the door of his room. The missionaries' home, like many of the homes in the region, was made of concrete blocks, painted in florescent colors. Between the eves of the roof and the top of the wall was a one-foot gap, which made way for cooling drafts of fresh air. The birds, having made nests under the eves, flew freely in and out of the house. Every window and door of the home was enhanced by elaborate steel bars. Mark actually liked the look, other than the fact that it was a telltale of how common place robbery was among the people.

Everyone else in the house was still asleep. Mark decided to wander out into the yard and look around. As he traced the perimeter wall of the property, he happened upon a tree, which, he concluded, must have been a fig tree. As he studied the interesting plant, he noticed long thin cactus growing among the branches. He meandered to the front gate. Looking down the road toward the valley where the village lay, he whispered under his breath, "This place is amazing." As the sun peaked over the horizon, spreading its morning light over the valley, Mark sat down and talked to the Lord about the things on his mind.

Later that day Erica asked if Mark would be interested in walking with her and her two daughters to the pueblo in the valley. They needed to buy some food. "It'd be a chance for you to see more of the culture ... and help us carry the groceries!" she said with a laugh. Mark was eager to go. It was about a two mile walk to town. Going was easy enough – downhill, and virtually nothing to carry. It was coming back up that would be the challenge. As they walked, Mark noted the different sights around him. An old man carrying a machete, leading his mule up further into the mountain to work the land. A bicycle, overloaded with two smiling boys, plus the one peddling. A Toyota truck with the driver's head poking out the side window because the windshield was too cracked to see out.

As they walked further into the town many notable smells, some pleasant, and some repulsive, evoked Mark's attention. A bakery, advertising delicious Pandebono cheese bread and other Colombian specialties . . . a fishery, proudly displaying wretched smelling seafood . . . an alley, littered with garbage and sewage . . . freshly made soup and tacos, sold at a portable wooden table on wheels . . . bouquets of flowers, being carried through the street on a cart while the seller called out to passers by.

Erica stopped to buy from a few local vegetable vendors, and then went into the grocery store to get the remaining supplies on her list. Mark loved the way she interacted with the people. So friendly and loving. By the time she finished at the store, Mark and the two girls each had something to carry. Just as they were about to head back home, Erica remembered, "Oh, I forgot to buy masa. That's the special corn flour we use for making tortillas and gorditas. Mark, do you mind staying here with the girls while I go in and get some?"

"No, that's fine."

Mark and the two girls waited on the brick sidewalk, holding the grocery bags. Just then a man in a motorized tricycle taxi pulled up next to them. He rattled off something in Spanish and motioned for them to get in. Mark looked at the girls, not knowing what to say.

"He thinks we're standing here because we need a ride," Bekah, the older daughter said. Then she responded to the driver in Spanish, gesturing with her hands that they weren't waiting for a ride. The driver looked disappointed and sped away down the street. "I guess we shouldn't stand so close to the street," she concluded.

Erica came back out with the masa, and the four started the trek back to the house. "I really like how people seem so laid back here," Mark commented. "It's like they have a completely different mindset and way of life than we do in the U.S. Here they are so relaxed and friendly."

"Yeah, it's true," Erica agreed. "They tend to live life one hour at a time and not worry about all the things that could 'need' to be done. Relationships – people – are more important than accomplishing a certain amount of work. I found out pretty quickly after moving here that rigid schedules are mostly non-existent."

"Was that hard for you to adjust to?"

"Yeah, it took me a while. Sometimes I found it frustrating. But God used these people to teach me a lesson about being too busy. Our culture in the States pushes us to pack our schedules full of so much work and activities that we don't have time to think, rest, or spend time with family. And that's not healthy. Now that we've been here a while I am slowly learning how to live with a healthy balance . . . and to treasure the time I spend with someone 'doing nothing' but investing in the relationship."

"Buenos Dias!" A woman greeted as they passed by her little hut of a home. She was washing laundry by hand in her outdoor washing station. Erica explained as they continued, that this washing area is where the family bathed, as well as washed clothes, fruits and vegetables.

"Do you know the family?"

"Yeah. Remember Manuel? Dad said you met him the other night at the get-together," Bekah began.

"Oh yeah."

"That's his house. That lady is his mom."

"Actually," Erica said throwing her bags of groceries over her shoulder for a different position, "we might go over there later today to help her with a project. Their family often doesn't have money for food, so we offered to help her get a garden started where she can grow some fresh vegetables. The first step will be to cut down the weeds so we can break up the ground."

"I could do that," Mark said willingly. "What kind of tools will we have?"

"I'll bring a machete," she responded demonstrating with her hands as if she were cutting down weeds. "I've learned since moving here, that tool is handy for so many things!"

Mark looked back toward Manuel's house and smiled. "Sounds like a plan!"

Chapter Eleven

*E*very day since Mark and Pete landed in Colombia had been meaningful. There was plenty to do, whether it was assisting with kids club, building and repairing things around the house, helping neighbors like Manuel and his family, handing out tracts in the town square, or traveling up the mountain to reach families in rural areas. Mark enjoyed helping at Manuel's house. Although he couldn't speak the boy's language, they found ways to communicate without words. Manuel looked up to Mark and loved the positive attention this strong American man gave to him. One day, when Manuel looked troubled, Mark tried to ask what was wrong, but the boy couldn't explain. So the two sat down and a tear trickled down Manuel's face as "the strong American man" prayed aloud for him. He didn't understand the words, but he understood the heart behind the words. *People need* *love . . . no matter what part of the world they live in.* Mark pondered. *People everywhere are starving for true love, that ultimately comes from God. What a blessing it is to bring God's love to people.*

It was Saturday morning – a week since leaving Alabama. Ed's family had one last ministry venture to share with Pete and Mark. They would load a bunch of Bibles into a truck they rented for the day and head up the mountain. At about 8:30 a.m. everything was ready and they all piled in . . . or on. Ed, Erica, and the girls managed to fit in the cab, while Mark and Pete chose to stretch their legs in the spacious bed of the truck. This ride was luxurious! During the past week, they had seen trucks loaded with three times this number of people.

Every so often Ed would pull over and all but two of the team would hop out and follow a trail or footpath to a home hidden away in the lush mountain. There they would visit, sing songs for the family, leave them with a little toy for the children, and most importantly, a Spanish Bible. Mark was astounded at the utter poverty of some of the homes. An 8 x 10 foot shack was home to a family with three young children. No kitchen, no bathroom. Only a twin-sized mattress on the floor, some sort of fire stove in one corner, a small table, and some hooks and shelves on the wall that held their few possessions.

An old man with shaky hands, rough from hard work, held the Bible that Mark gave him. Then the man explained his dilemma to Ed: he couldn't read. Ed offered to come once a week and read it aloud with him. Many sad and joyful things had reached the old ears of this man, but nothing compared to the Good News Ed shared with him today. He wanted to know more about the Savior.

At another home farther up the mountain Mark met Hilda and her son Alejandro. This precious elderly lady seemed not to notice her lack of possessions. Mark observed as Erica offered her a Bible as a gift. She didn't take it, but instead excitedly ran over to her bed and picked up a worn book, waving it in the air. "La Biblia es mi vida!" she proclaimed joyfully. *The Bible is my life!* Somewhere, she had already obtained a copy. This poverty-stricken woman possessed one precious book that made her spiritually rich.

The mission for the day was both rewarding, and exhausting. That evening as they drove back down the mountain, Mark thought about the opportunities he'd had in the past week to tell people about the Savior. It had been great, in spite of the language barrier which was a bit of a hindrance. He hearkened back to the times he had helped the Kallenbachs share the gospel at events in the States. Millions of people around the world need to hear the gospel, but so few Christians are willing to share it. He himself had fallen in that category not long ago. Mark imagined Jerome standing next to the old man with shaky hands. There are people, not only in third-world countries, but in the *United States*, that have lived their entire lives, not knowing how to be saved. The United States needs missionaries, whether it be simply Christians witnessing in their workplace, or full-time missionaries and evangelists. Mark felt a tug on his heart. *Lord, do you want me to stay in the U.S. as a missionary?*

Pressing Toward the Mark

"That was quite the week, and I'm tired out!" Hannah said as she unpacked things from their gospel booth.

"Do you feel like things went pretty well overall?" Her mom was collecting the remaining tracts and dividing them into stacks of about 100. "I thought things went pretty smoothly, myself."

The twins came skipping into the dining room where their mom and sister were working. "Mom, can we help?" Jed asked with the most irresistible excitement.

Phillip was just as enthusiastic. "Yeah, can we stack some tracks?"

Mrs. Kallenbach smiled at the way the boys always said that word: "tracks." "Um, let's see." She thought for a second about what she could let them "help" with. "You guys can put rubber bands on the stacks of tracts I'm making. Here, like this." She helped them with a couple stacks. The five-year-olds struggled a little at first, but this gave Mrs. Kallenbach time to divide more stacks for them to bind.

Hannah's mind lingered on her mom's question. "It was pretty amazing hearing from Grace and Zack about the conversation they had with that guy and his girlfriend. It's not very often that we talk to someone that open and ready to receive the gospel."

"Yes, praise the Lord! That made all of our efforts at the fair worth it," Mrs. Kallenbach commented.

"Sometimes, Mom, it seems like the majority of Americans have already heard about Christ and the Cross... they're just too busy or proud to accept and believe Him personally."

"I know what you mean, but there still are a few who haven't heard, or who want to learn more, like that young couple."

"Yeah," Phillip piped up, "and some kids, like Jed and my's age don't know even nothing about the Bible!"

A smile spread across Hannah's face at the cuteness and sincerity of her little brother. "You're right Phillip." She looked at her mother again. "Don't get me wrong, Mom. I know that even one person receiving the gospel is something to celebrate. I'm really thankful. But sometimes I wonder if our ministry would be more effective in another country... where they haven't had so much exposure to the gospel. Like, if we spent a week sharing the gospel like we just did at the fair - just in another place - would we see maybe *ten* people get saved, rather than one?"

"I see your point, Hannah," Mrs. Kallenbach said contemplatively, "and if it's God's will for you to share the gospel in another country, then He surely has plans for you there, and you should follow His leading. But if He's placed you here for the time being, He has a very specific reason for that. There are lost souls here too, who are searching for the truth. Someone needs to be here to tell them about Christ."

Hannah gazed far away out the window. "I know you're right. Even if there's just one searching person here that God wants me to point to Christ, I will be glad to stay." She glanced at her mom's neat stacks of tracts on the table. The twins had lost interest in banding them together, and were now trying to shoot each other with the rubber bands. "I guess I shouldn't look at success in terms of numbers," she concluded. "It's not my responsibility to report huge numbers of people saved every year. It's my responsibility to be faithful and diligent in the work God has given me. The results are in His hands."

Hannah would never know on this side of heaven, the full impact of their witness at the fair that previous week. To her it seemed only a handful of people had been interested. But did she have any idea that the teen-aged boy she had given a tract to could not sleep that night, because he was wrestling about the destiny of his soul? Did she know that the tatoo-covered woman who had mocked her for being there had later gone home, read the tract, and burst into uncontrollable tears as she realized for the first time that Christ died out of love for her? Did Hannah ever imagine that a fellow believer who had seen them witnessing from across the street had been so convicted and challenged, that he committed his life to full-time ministry? No. She did not know, and she didn't need to know. Just as she said, she only needed to faithfully serve the Lord and leave the results up to Him.

Hi Grace! Greetings from Colombia! Mark's email began.

Today is our eighth day here. Looks like it will be couple of days before we head back to the States. Because Pete flies for a commercial airline, he was able to get some cheap last minute flights for us.

My time here has been amazing . . . hard to put into words all that God has been teaching me!

I no longer have this unrealistic, movie-set idea of a tropical mission field, but I've personally seen what it's like. There are some wonderful things about it, and some downright ugly things that go on down here. I wonder if it's anything like Hannah imagines it to be.

Mark stopped for a minute, and then deleted the last sentence about Hannah.

I've walked the streets, dug in the dirt, gotten hot and dirty, played with the children, talked with the people, experienced the real thing. And it's just that – so REAL. At first some of the homes, and the way of life I saw here seemed strange, but now, just eight days later, I wonder why it seemed so strange before.

Colombia is a country with a lot of internal turmoil. The people here have suffered from decades of conflict between rebel groups (like the FARC - Revolutionary Armed Forces of Colombia) and the paramilitary. Heavy drug trafficking contributes to the problem on both sides. The missionaries here say that even though a few years ago the FARC surrendered to the Colombian government, there are still many members who have regrouped. Fortunately this region where Ed and Erica live is not in the "red zone" where it is much more dangerous.

A few things I have seen or experienced here will be forever etched in my memory, even if I never come back:

- *Men trotting their horses down the cobblestone streets*
- *The little children curiously peering thru the bars of the house porch window, or standing in the doorway quietly observing us as we pass.*
- *The trucks driving around town with loudspeakers announcing pre-recorded news, info, advertisements, and music*
- *The delicious food – Mogolla bread, tamales, carimañolas, and more. (Erica has learned to cook all the traditional foods here, and sometimes the neighbor lady comes over and they cook their meals together.)*
- *Looking forward to telling you all about it when I see you! I have so much to tell you, not only about this trip, but about my journey this past summer.*

But this will have to do for now.

Love,

Mark

"Oh dear!" Erica snapped her fingers. "I knew we were forgetting something when we went down to the pueblo for groceries last time!"

Mark popped his head around the doorway into the kitchen. "What did we forget?"

"I was going to get some balloons for the kids' Bible program tonight."

"I can run into town and pick it up for you," Mark offered.

"No, you don't have to do that. Besides, I wouldn't want to send you alone."

Mark looked back over his shoulder into the living room. "Pete, you want to run an errand with me?"

"Sure, why not?" Pete stood setting aside the guitar he had been playing around with.

Erica was about to protest further but Mark insisted. "We've been to town with you a few times, and I think we know our way around, somewhat at least. It can't be that complicated to buy a few balloons, can it?"

"Okay, it *would* be really helpful for you guys to pick them up. Just be careful. I'll give you directions to the store."

The two-mile walk from the missionaries' home to the pueblo was one Mark wished he could experience every day. It was so relaxing. So beautiful. So peaceful.

When he and Pete reached the colorful little general store which Erica had told them about, it didn't take them long to locate the balloons. Pete offered to do the talking at the register since he knew more Spanish than Mark. After making their purchase, the two men stepped back out onto the street. Something told Mark there were eyes watching them. He wondered if Pete could sense it too. But nah, he reasoned, as white-skinned Americans he and Pete stood out from the crowd. Of course people were watching them. What he didn't see though was the three men following them in camouflage with AK-47 rifles slung over their shoulders.

As they neared the edge of the pueblo, Mark glanced at his watch. "Well, it's only 2:30. We'll have these balloons to Erica in plenty of time before the kids' program tonight."

Up ahead about 100 feet a rusty Toyota Tacoma pickup sat on the edge of the road. It reminded Mark of a truck he had owned as a teenager, only this one looked like it had lived through three lifetimes. Mark's thoughts were abruptly interrupted as two men stepped out from behind the truck with AK-47s pointed right at them.

"Stop right there!" one of them said with a thick Spanish accent. Mark and Pete could hear rapid footsteps approaching from behind.

"We have you surrounded. Don't try any tricks."

Mark's heart was pounding. He could feel adrenaline coursing through his veins. He glanced at Pete, wondering if he felt equally taken off guard. Pete looked relatively calm and collected. Everything seemed to be happening in slow motion, yet at the same time, too quickly to know how to react.

Two of the men from behind grabbed Pete and Mark's hands, tying them securely behind their backs. Then suddenly everything became black as the captors put dark hoods over their heads.

Mark wanted to ask who they were and why they were doing this, but he had heard stories of how merciless and barbaric the guerrillas and drug lords could be, and he wanted to make it home alive. He suddenly felt the cold circular end of a rifle held to his back and someone growled at Mark and Pete to walk forward. Could this really be happening? They were marched over to the pickup truck which Mark had noticed just moments before the attack. It had a makeshift canvass canopy over the bed of the truck, slightly resembling some sort of military vehicle. "Get in!" a gruff voice demanded, and the captives scrambled up into the truck bed with the help of a shove. At least two people climbed in after them. The truck rumbled to a start and soon Mark and Pete could feel the roughness of the road on which they were traveling. The fact that the hoods over their faces kept them from seeing anything, as well as restricted them from breathing much fresh air, only intensified their confusion.

The truck rattled it's way southeast across Valle del Cauca. Mark's stomach began to feel nauseous. Where were they taking them? Finally, after what seemed like hours, the sickening movement stopped and the men could hear the truck's engine shut off. Doors slammed. Mark felt a tug on his arm. "Vamanos!" One of the captors yelled. Mark scooted to the edge of the truck bed and jumped down. Pete came right behind him. With one abrupt swoosh, the hoods were snatched off. Mark's eyes tried to adjust to the afternoon light. The road they were stopped on looked familiar. Was it the long driveway to the mission headquarters?

For the first time the captives got a good look at their captors. A very short, burly man in his 50's addressed them. He didn't look too intimidating at a glance, but his eyes were piercing with a hardened, desperately wicked darkness about them. Mark felt a shiver down his spine.

Pressing Toward the Mark

The man smiled slyly. "I am called Bruto. You will both work for me now," he began with a thick Spanish accent. "Either you will fly your plane for us and make deliveries of cocaine, or your rich American friends can send ransom money and we will release you."

Mark and Pete were putting two and two together. These drug runners thought both of them were pilots.

Bruto continued. "Our first job for you starts today. One of you will fly your lovely new mission plane to another location. Which one of you will volunteer?"

Pete spoke up quickly. "I will. I am more experienced. Mark is just my co-pilot."

That's strange. I wonder why he called me his co-pilot, rather than telling them I can't fly. He must have a plan. Mark wished he could read Pete's mind.

"Ok," Bruto said satisfied. "You will go with Fernando and Raul, and I will take him back to camp," he said pointing to Mark.

Mark wished he and Pete could stay together. If they got separated, they might never see each other again, nor know what happened to the other. He couldn't think of any way to avoid it though.

Bruto stared Pete in the eye, getting close so that his breath almost made Pete choke. "If you and that plane are not at the camp by the time I arrive in the truck, we will kill him," he said, referring to Mark.

Pressing Toward the Mark

Fernando and Raul led Pete away through the thick underbrush toward the mission hanger. Mark was loaded back onto the truck and the bumpy ride began again.

Pete's footsteps were hurried as he and the two guerrilla's approached the hangar. He wished there was some way he could get the attention of someone at the mission. He had to stay calm and clear headed. He prayed for peace, and God supplied it. His captors kept such a close eye on him. There was no opportunity to get help or to escape. They assisted Pete in pushing the airplane out of the hanger. After the pre-flight check, the captive and his captors climbed into the plane.

Pete glanced out the window in he direction of the mission headquarters. If only someone would notice the plane just now! The engine roared to life. After completing the run-up, Pete taxied out to the runway, pushed the throttle forward, and started the takeoff roll. The Cessna gently lifted off the pavement, and the mission headquarters became smaller and smaller. Pete felt a knot forming in his stomach. He wished he could get help somehow. That might have been his only opportunity to be in civilization for a long time. Getting help would only get harder as they headed further into the the bush. He thought for a moment about trying to get a radio transmission out without his captors noticing. But no, they were too attentive at the moment. For fear that these AK-47 armed men might catch on, Pete decided not to try anything just yet.

Pressing Toward the Mark

As they continued flying toward the guerrilla camp the pilot kept brainstorming, and an idea started to form in his mind. As long as Mark didn't tell anyone that he wasn't a pilot, it might work . . . just maybe.

The Toyota pick-up worked its way deeper and deeper into the Colombian mountains. It had been almost three hours since they had left Pete near the mission hangar. Land travel was extremely slow in these remote areas. The roads were mostly gravel; or mud with deep ruts where rain had washed away what little bit of road had previously been there. An occasional stream flowed across the rugged road, and fallen trees and debris often called for an off-road detour. The sun was near setting when the truck finally came to a halt and the men piled out. Mark was led down a narrow footpath through the jungle underbrush until they reached a large opening where about 20 other rebels were gathered. Most of the group were men, but there were at least three or four women among them. Mark scanned the camp, hoping to see Pete among the others. It was a busy place: miniature tarp shelters strung between trees, a good-sized fire with a pot of boiling water above it, and a few make-shift log benches placed in a circle. There was even a small Colombian style outdoor "kitchen" where a few women were preparing food. It looked like the group had stationed themselves here for more than a few days. Mark was relieved when he spotted Pete sitting at the base of a tree on the other side of the camp. Of course, it had taken Pete less time to fly there than it did for Mark and the others to travel by truck through the mountains.

After tying Mark and Pete to trees on opposite sides of the camp, the guerrillas gathered around the fire and had their fill of rice and beans. They didn't bother to share any with their prisoners.

The night seemed to drag on endlessly. By the time the first hints of dawn appeared Mark's hands and arms felt numb from being cramped behind him for so many hours. He felt weak and exhausted. Activity began early in the camp. The women started fires and fixed some breakfast. The men made plans for the day. Mark and Pete were so thankful for the small amount of food they received that morning to calm the hollow feeling in their stomachs. Just as Mark was taking his last bite, one of the gang members came over and addressed him. "Bruto said to untie you. Don't try to run or we will shoot you."

"Gracias!" Mark was so relieved. He never imagined how uncomfortable and downright painful it could be to have your hands tied for an entire night. He glanced over in Pete's direction. Good. They were cutting the rope off of his hands too.

Bruto gathered everyone into a circle to give directives. Much of what he said was in Spanish, but when he addressed Mark and Pete he switched to English.

"You!" he said switching abruptly and pointing at Pete. "You will walk with my men to our airstrip and help unload the truck when they come with more cocaine. And you . . ." he said referring to Mark, "stay and help the women with things here." He apparently didn't want Pete and Mark working together.

After most of the men had gone down the wooded path to the airstrip, Mark was put to work helping to hand-wash laundry and cook food for lunch with the women. With his limited knowledge of Spanish, he felt like his hands were tied when it came to communicating with these people. Pete was good at interpreting as well as he could for his friend, but for the time being, Mark was on his own.

A subset of the guerrillas had piled into the truck and driven away around the same time that the others had gone to the airstrip. Mark wondered what kinds of things kept these people busy all day. On second thought, maybe he didn't want to know.

As Mark attempted to build a good fire for cooking, he noticed two guerrilla women chattering in Spanish a few paces away. They were obviously criticizing his work. "¡El gringo no sabe nada!" The older of the two women marched over and snatched the piece of wood out of Mark's hand. Mark stood to his feet and stepped back, allowing her to take over. He watched her intrigued. He wasn't that poor at starting fires, but this woman was a professional, if there was such a thing. Within a few minutes, she had a blazing, sustained fire going. She turned to Mark, folded her arms, and smirked with a twinkle in her eye. He wanted to say he was impressed, but he didn't know the Spanish words. "Wow," he said, giving two thumbs up.

The group that had left earlier in the truck returned a little before the midday meal. Mark noticed two new faces among them. A boy around the age of 16 and a girl a couple years

Pressing Toward the Mark

older. They looked like Colombians but not rebel guerrillas. Mark wondered what their story was. The newcomers were brought before Bruto and Fernando, who was second in command, for introductions.

Over lunch Mark and Pete were able to sit next to each other for the first time since being captured, but were still being watched closely. Their meal was a bowl of traditional Colombian soup called Sancocho. In spite of the very tough wild boar meat in it, the soup was very tasty. It had a variety of starches, vegetables and seasonings including potatoes, cassava, plantains, onions, cilantro, and cumin.

"Are you doing okay?" Pete asked.

"Yeah, kind of." Mark wasn't sure. "How about you?" He glanced at the gang members just a few paces away. No, they couldn't talk about escape right now. Every word they said could be heard.

When the meal was finished Bruto stood up and gathered everyone's attention. "Camaradas," he began, addressing his men, "I want to introduce you to our newest team members." He motioned to the boy and girl to stand up. "Maria and Marco are cousins. Both of their families were killed by the paramilitary, and, like us, they want revenge!"

The whole group of rebels shouted with passion, raising their fists in the air.

Bruto continued. "Today they met our men and have decided to join our band."

With a gesture from Bruto, the youngsters proceeded to go around the circle shaking hands with each of the guerrillas.

Pressing Toward the Mark

For the first time since coming to Colombia, Mark started to understand why so many guerrillas were so dedicated to fighting and shedding blood. Their reason wasn't a good reason, nevertheless he could see the anger and emotional pain written all over so many faces. *Lord, as long as I'm here, I want to be used by you to reach these people. Some of them seem so calloused and dead to any feeling at all, but Your love can penetrate in where nothing else can.*

When the boy and girl had concluded their round of handshakes, Bruto took the stage again. He loved to hear himself talk and give orders. "Also, we now have the privilege of having our own pilot and his assistant." Everyone looked at Mark and Pete. "Almost all of the cocaine for the big sale has been delivered here. Tomorrow our new pilots will help you load the cocaine into the plane and then Fernando and I will fly with one of them to Valle de Espinas to finalize the deal with our contacts. This will be a multi-million dollar sale. Let's celebrate with drinks and music!"

A cheer erupted from the group and they dispersed to bring out the beer and turn on some loud music.

Mark wrestled with the thought of being involved with a drug transaction. Pete's mind was developing a plan of action.

Chapter Twelve

"Charlie, this is Ed Winston calling from Colombia," the stressed missionary began. "We have a problem. As you know, Pete and Mark have been staying with us for the past week and a half. And . . . well I'll just say it plainly. Mark and Pete went missing yesterday afternoon while they were in town doing an errand."

Charlie groaned, running his fingers through his hair.

"We don't know for sure what happened. Later in the evening our mission director at the headquarters called me and said the airplane had been stolen from the hangar. We think the men may have been abducted by a guerrilla group and forced to fly the plane for them."

Charlie sat silently on the other end of the call. What should they even do?

Ed continued. "I've notified the police and they are on the lookout for them and the plane. But with the endless acres of wild mountains and countryside around here, it could take forever for the police to track them down."

"So is there anything we can do?"

"It's fairly likely the guerrillas will be in touch with the Colombian government soon, demanding a ransom for the two men. If it comes to that, then we'll have to consider our options."

"And if we don't hear from them?"

"Well, if we don't hear anything, there's nothing we can do but wait and pray."

Charlie sighed heavily. "I can call Mark's family if you'd like."

"Yes, thank you. I should let you go so I can try calling Pete's family again."

"Alright, thanks for the call, Ed."

"Sure. And remember to keep trusting God. He is with our friends, wherever they are."

"You're right. Thanks for the reminder. Let me know if you hear anything new."

"Will do, Brother."

Charlie ended the call and walked slowly to the bedroom where his wife was putting away laundry. "Sarah, I need to tell you about the very serious phone call I just had with Ed Winston."

Pressing Toward the Mark

The two sat on the edge of the bed and Charlie explained the situation. After spending a few moments in prayer they decided to call Grace.

Grace was stunned by the news. She didn't know what to do or say. When she had finished the phone call she immediately called her husband at work. She thought about calling the Kallenbachs too. But how would Hannah take the news? Maybe she should just keep the news to herself for a while. No, that was silly. Besides, the more people praying for Mark and his pilot friend the better. Grace marched out to her car and drove the short distance to the Kallenbach farm. She had to tell them.

Mark awoke with a kick in his side. "Get up, Lazy!" Fernando was not in the least bit patient. Mark scrambled to his feet, feeling a little dizzy from getting up so quickly. That's right, today was the big drug deal day. He wasn't sure what to expect. As Fernando marched him and Pete down the path to the airstrip he prayed for the Lord's protection and direction. When they entered the clearing they could see that the new cousins and a few other men were already carting over stacks of cocaine from the shack on the edge of the airstrip.

Fernando didn't waste any time. "Gringos, start loading this cocaine into the plane. Hurry! I think a storm is coming." Reluctantly, the men obeyed. The two commanders walked back to the camp, leaving another man to keep an eye on the gringos.

When they were out of sight, Pete started a conversation with his guard in Spanish. "In preparation for our flight I should really see a weather report. Do you have a radio, or a cell phone I could use to check?" Halfway through his sentence he realized there was no way they would allow that to happen. His brow furrowed. The sky was looking more ominous with every minute. A storm was certainly brewing. He'd have to make do without a weather report.

Pete moved on to ask the guard other important information about the flight. He asked about the total weight of cocaine they wanted to load into the airplane. He asked about the distance to their destination, so he could calculate the amount of fuel he would need to fly there. Finally he explained that he needed to take a look at some charts in the plane's P.O.H (Pilot's Operating Handbook). He wanted to verify how much weight he could load the plane with, taking into account the length of the airstrip, and the density altitude. The guard went with him to the front of the plane and watched as Pete made his calculations. The full weight of the cargo . . . plus himself . . . and Mark . . . and probably both Bruto and Fernando would go . . . then fuel weight. It would be quite a loaded plane! Would he need to have full fuel tanks? No, it wasn't that far to Valle de Espinas, and even less distance to the La Vista. He was glad he had looked the night before during his flight to the camp to see where the nearest airports were located. The regional airport at La Vista would fit into his scheme well. The weight should be okay, as long as he left with the fuel tanks no more than half full. He checked the fuel gauges. He had about a quarter of the fuel left. It would be enough. Pete stepped down from the door on the side of the plane and spoke to the man again. "Okay, I need to give the men instructions on how to load the plane and distribute the weight."

The men loading were cooperative and with so many hands helping, it didn't take long to finish the project. Pete walked from the side of the Cessna where they were loading the main cabin, over to the baggage compartments in the nose of the plane. His guard hung back a ways and chatted with one of the others. Mark was fastening shut one of the nose compartments when Pete came to inspect.

Mark chuckled. "Never thought I'd help load up a plane with illegal drugs!"

"Never thought I'd fly one!" was Pete's comeback. Pete's face returned to serious as he mumbled under his breath, "Do they still think you can fly?"

"Yes."

"Good." Pete nodded covertly and continued to work.

Shortly after the loading was complete, Bruto and Fernando appeared on the scene again.

"Okay," Bruto instructed. "You go back with my men to the camp," he said looking at Mark.

"And you," he said addressing Pete, "get in the plane and take me and Fernando to Valle de Espinas."

"Oh, but I have to have my co-pilot!" Pete said premeditatedly.

"Co-pilot? You flew the plane yourself yesterday."

Pressing Toward the Mark

"Yes, but that was a very short distance. It's definitely not safe to fly all the way to Valle de Espinas with only one pilot, especially with this heavy load." Pete tried to look serious.

Fernando looked unsure.

Bruto was not yet convinced.

Mark came to Pete's aid. "And with this bad storm moving in," Mark looked up at the dark clouds, "he especially needs a co-pilot."

"Are you sure you need him to come along, and that it's unsafe to go without him?" Bruto asked Pete one more time.

"Yes, absolutely." Pete looked confidently at Mark. Yes, his friend definitely needed to come along, but for Mark's sake, not theirs. And it was certainly unsafe to go without him . . . unsafe for Mark, not for them.

"Alright, then he can go," the commander finally agreed.

This plan just might work, Pete thought to himself.

The drug laden airplane cut its way through the humid Colombian air. Mark looked at Pete sitting to his left. What was his plan? He seemed to be in concentrated thought. Their captors were still very attentive, sitting sideways in the rear-facing seats just behind the cockpit. Their AK-47 rifles lay across their laps, ready to be used on a whim.

Pete debated within himself whether he should try to communicate something to Mark through the intercom. Bruto and Fernando were too alert just now for that. Maybe further into the flight they would relax a little. Pete reached down and discreetly typed four numbers into the transponder: 7.5.0.0. This squawk code would alert anyone watching the radar that his aircraft was being hijacked. The question was, was there any radar in that area? He had flown in many areas before where there was no radar.

It was now just before noon. They had been in flight for about 45 minutes. Still no sign of being seen on radar by air traffic control. The two guerrillas had turned around in their seats to face the back for a more comfortable ride. Pete switched the intercom to crew mode so that only Mark could hear when he spoke through his headset.

"Mark, can you hear me?" he asked still looking straight ahead so as to not attract the attention of the men sitting behind him.

"Affirmative."

"We are going to do an emergency landing when the plane appears to be malfunctioning. If the airport received my message they will be ready for us."

"Ok," Mark said, not fully understanding the plan.

Pete thought about what might happen if he made an emergency landing and the squawk code was never picked up by radar. The airport would not understand his situation, and they would not be ready. But at least he and Mark would be on the ground, and others would be watching. The guerrillas

Pressing Toward the Mark

could try to hold them as hostages, but what did they have to lose? He and Mark were already captives.

Pete's heart leaped as he heard air traffic control over the radio indicating that his distress code had been seen. "Unidentified aircraft ten miles southeast of La Vista, confirming squawking 7500?" The controller wanted to verify that the pilot had intentionally sent the hijack distress code.

"Affirmative," Pete replied on the radio. He looked at his GPS location. They would be coming up on La Vista Airport in just a few minutes.

When he could see the runway ahead, Pete made eye contact with Mark, trying signal without words for him to play along. He knew that with two simple steps he could set off the gear warning horn, which is designed to alert a pilot that the landing gear is not down when he is about to land. With a slick move of the hand he discretely adjusted the flaps of the Cessna to extend. Then he brought the power lever back a bit causing the plane to slow down and descend rapidly. Immediately a loud, urgent beeping sounded in the cockpit, drawing everyone's attention to the front. Pete tried to look nervous. "Mark, it looks like we've got a problem with one of the engines."

"Yes, I see! I think our only choice is to land, isn't it?"

"Absolutely."

"What is that beeping?" Bruto demanded, turning around in his seat. His face showed alarm.

Pete switched the intercom to cabin mode so that the two guerrillas, as well as Air Traffic Control could hear him.

"Bruto and Fernando, there is a dangerous problem with one of the airplane's engines, and we have to make an emergency landing. Please buckle your seatbelts and stay calm. Once we land, exit the plane quickly in case there is a fire."

Pete knew there was no turning back now. He had made the decision to land and he hoped it was a good one. There were so many questions in his mind. Most of all, what would happen after they landed? Mark wondered the same thing.

Bruto attempted to stand up and analyze the situation with a greater sense of control. "Land?! You can't land until we arrive in Valle de Espinas!"

Pete gave the flight controls a little shove, sending the plane in a short dive. Bruto's head hit the ceiling, and he stumbled back into the seat holding his hand on his head.

Fernando's face was growing more serious with each second. He watched as Pete and Mark frantically checked their instruments. Pete handed Mark the airplane's operating handbook, and Mark fingered through it as if looking for some emergency procedure. The pilot continued to intentionally handle the airplane roughly, stepping on the rudder pedals and moving the controls around, all the while acting as though flying was taking all of his effort.

"Where are you going to land?" Fernando finally managed to ask as he gripped the back of his seat.

"I see a place I can land just ahead," Pete said.

Bruto stood up again, shoving the end of his rifle barrel against Pete's side. "Escuchame Piloto! Listen! This better not be a trap or I will kill you!"

Pressing Toward the Mark

The incessant beeping of the gear warning horn, combined with the apparent distress of the pilots was putting everyone on edge. Fernando was convinced something was legitimately wrong with the plane. "Comandante," he said, addressing Bruto, "I think we have to land or the plane will crash!"

Pete spoke over the intercom again. "Please fasten your seatbelts, and get ready for a rough landing."

Fernando had already done so. Bruto plopped down into his seat again and did what the pilot instructed. He didn't like being controlled. However, if this plane really was having problems, he wanted to make it out of there alive. As much as he tried to hide it, fear was starting to grip him.

Pete switched the intercom back to crew/ATC mode and made initial contact with La Vista Airport. "MAYDAY, MAYDAY, MAYDAY. La Vista Tower, Cessna November-Four-Eight-Niner-Two is fives miles southeast, landing runway One-Four, squawking 7500."

"Cessna November-Four-Eight-Niner-Two, cleared to land. Are you squawking 7500?" the controller asked again, confirming that it was a hijack situation.

"Affirmative," Pete replied. "Squawking 7500. Cleared to land."

At the last possible moment, Pete put the landing gear down and the beeping stopped. For a few minutes no one inside the plane said a word. For one reason or another, all four men feared for their lives.

Pete continued his pretense that the airplane was difficult to fly. He added to the validity of the emergency by adjusting

Pressing Toward the Mark

the propeller control so that the engine appeared to be misbehaving.

He pulled the controls back sooner than usual, intentionally landing with a slightly uncomfortable "plop." He didn't like mistreating the airplane, but he knew his life depended on his captors being convinced of a malfunctioning engine. As soon as the aircraft was on the ground, but before it was slowed, he turned off the runway and towards the ramp as aggressively as he dared. He maneuvered the aircraft towards the terminal building, not braking until he was just in front of it.

La Vista was a regional airport with not a large amount of air traffic. And at this moment all eyes were on the Cessna 402 that had just landed. As the airplane came to a full stop, fire trucks and law enforcement vehicles moved in quickly around it.

Pete promptly shut down the engine and gave his captors instructions. "Get out quickly," he said, sounding urgent. "You don't want to be inside of the plane if one of those engines blows up!"

Bruto and Fernando hesitated. They glanced at their AK-47s and then out the window at the law enforcement now surrounding the plane. They didn't know for sure what was going on, but they hoped the police were there simply because of the engine emergency. If not, they were in big trouble.

"Look," Bruto said, pulling a small pistol out of his coat and discreetly holding it to Pete's side, "You pretend like we are your friends. Do NOT let them search the plane." Then he motioned for Fernando to hide their rifles somewhere in the plane.

Moments later, as the four men exited the airplane, officers leveled their guns on them, and the four men raised their hands without any physical resistance.

Bruto protested, playing the part of an innocent victim. "I-I don't know what this is about. Our plane just had a problem and we had to land. But my pilot friends here will be able to fix it right away and we will go!"

Everyone seemed to ignore what he had to say. Soon Bruto, Fernando, Pete, and Mark were all handcuffed and made to sit in the squelching hot police vehicles while a thorough search of the Cessna was conducted. It would take some time to get this situation sorted out. Pete and Mark were confident they would released, even if it required spending some time at a Colombian police station first. The drug lords, however, would undoubtedly be imprisoned.

Chapter Thirteen

"Hannah," Grace said waving her friend over, "your brother Charlie is calling my phone! Maybe he has an update on Mark and Pete!"

Hannah hurried over to the the kitchen table where her friend was working and listened as Grace answered the call. Grace put the phone on speaker so Hannah could hear.

"Hi Grace, I wanted to let you know that Ed Winston just called with good news," Charlie began. The two ladies exchanged smiles of relief. "It's a long story, but they found Mark and Pete, and they are unharmed."

"Thank God!" Grace sighed. Hannah nodded in agreement.

"They were abducted by a guerrilla group that is involved in the drug industry, and Pete was forced to fly the mission plane for them. Apparently he found a way to land at a different place than they were supposed to, and get help from law enforcement."

"Wow," Hannah commented, "I wish I could have been there when they landed! I can just imagine how upset the kidnappers were!"

"Yeah, it sounds like they were quite unhappy, but there was nothing they could do once they were surrounded by the police. Ed said these guys had been doing criminal activity in that area for years but had somehow managed to evade getting caught. It's about time they spend some time in jail!"

"I'd say so," Grace said emphatically.

Charlie continued. "Ed has been at the police station with Mark and Pete all day waiting for them to get things sorted out and get some paperwork filled out, but it sounds like they're almost done."

"Good!" Grace said thankfully.

"They're planning to go back to the Winstons, pack up, and catch a flight back home in the next couple of days.

Grace and Hannah were elated by the news - and relieved. Perhaps they could finally get some sleep tonight!

September rolled in just as quickly as Mark could blink an eye. His experiences in Colombia felt like an elaborate dream where time and anything normal didn't exist. Even though time seemed to stand still, the clock kept ticking back in the States. Now that he had returned to Alabama, it was time to make some plans. He and Charlie talked for hours discussing what Mark had learned in Colombia, and what God was putting on his heart for ministry. "There's one thing I don't like to admit, but it was a struggle that I had to surrender to the Lord," Mark explained one evening over supper. "As I said, I'm sensing God's call to do mission work in the United States. The thing is, I know that Hannah wants to be a foreign missionary . . . ."

Charlie's wife stopped chewing her food when he mentioned Hannah. *So he did still care for her.* She exchanged a look with Charlie and listened quietly as Mark continued.

"I thought a lot about this when I was on the mission trip, even before our run-in with the guerrillas. I'm not afraid of putting myself in danger again if God led me to go there. But I honestly believe God's place for me is here, not there on the foreign mission field. My decision is made. I want to obey God, no matter what the cost . . . even though that means giving up the hope of Hannah ever becoming my wife."

Charlie knew his sister well enough to know she wouldn't see it that way. "You're doing the right thing, Mark, and I'm glad you are willing to give up Hannah in order to serve the Lord. Do you realize that's the same thing she did?"

Mark looked confused.

"Hannah broke off the courtship because she didn't think the Lord was your first priority. Her desire is to serve God with her life, no matter what the cost – even though it meant giving up her relationship with you."

Pressing Toward the Mark

Mark nodded thoughtfully.

"And if you want to know what I think," Sarah said with a hint of playfulness in her voice, "there still is hope for you and Hannah. Her heart is set on ministry, but it may not have to be foreign ministry."

Mark stabbed his fork mindlessly into the salad on his plate. *Maybe she's right. But what about Jasper?* "Well, I don't know, Sarah. I think the possibility is pretty slim... especially if she has other options."

Sarah let out a quick chuckle. She didn't realize Mark thought Hannah was being pursued by someone else. Of course, she had never even heard about Jasper because he never was a serious possibility for Hannah.

"Just keep trusting God, Mark," Charlie counseled, "with every detail of your life."

For two weeks, Mark stayed with Charlie and Sarah, working odd jobs and helping with various ministries at their church.

On a cool morning, he met with the pastor in his living room.

"Pastor Hayes, I'd like help regularly with your visitation ministry... as long as I'm staying here in Alabama," he said clutching his Bible firmly in both hands.

"I would love that, Mark. Charlie has been a big blessing to me, but he travels a lot for ministry, and usually isn't available to help with visitation."

Mark nodded, and went on. "Remember how I told you about my friend Jerome, and how I failed to share the gospel with him before he died?"

"Yes."

"Well, God has taught me a hard lesson about being a faithful witness."

The pastor looked downward, nodding understandingly. Mark continued. "And He's been speaking to my heart about doing missions here in America. I've been praying about different ways to do that. The hospitals are full of people like Jerome who don't have long to live and need to hear the gospel. Helping you with visitation is one way I can reach out to them."

"Mark, what you're saying is true . . ." Pastor Hayes said calmly, lifting his head to look Mark in the eye, "but are you wanting to do this because you feel a sense of guilt? Are you feeling like you need to pay God back for your failure with Jerome?"

"No, it's really not that. I know God has forgiven me. Like it talks about in Philippians, I want to forget those things which are behind, and reach forward to those things which are before me. I am inspired, though, to reach people in hospitals whose lives are hanging in the balance."

The older gentleman's serious face softened into a genuine smile. "Then I think you're the perfect man to help me with visitation. I have plans to go to the hospital this Wednesday. Are you up to it?"

"Absolutely!"

Pressing Toward the Mark

Hannah handed Grace a milk bucket, and they began milking goats. The milk house was connected to the main barn where the rest of the goats were sheltered. Willie was enthusiastically spreading clean bedding for the does – his newest responsibility on the farm. He liked doing chores like one of the big kids. The twins and Heather Rose often "helped" with the animal chores and milking, but they didn't have any chores of their own yet. Grace and Hannah sat for a few minutes milking in thoughtful silence. Some days they chattered nonstop or had a bunch of little hands trying to help, but other days, like today, the constant rhythm of milk squirting into the buckets seemed almost mesmerizing. Their trains of thought were interrupted by the unmistakable sound of a diesel truck pulling into the driveway. Willie rushed to the barn door to see who had arrived.

"Guys," he said looking back at them with wide eyes, "it's Jasper!"

The two stopped milking and looked at each other.

"Dad's not home, so somebody else needs to go talk to him," Willie informed.

"I'm not going out there!" Hannah said quickly.

"Oh good, Daniel just came out of the house. I'm going to go listen to them talk." With that, Willie ran out, swinging the barn door shut behind him.

Pressing Toward the Mark

Hannah and Grace gave each other a mischievous look that they both understood. Setting their milk buckets aside they ran with hushed giggles to spy through the crack in the door.

"So is your sister Hannah here today?" Jasper was asking Daniel.

"Um . . . I'm not sure what she's up to at the moment," he said evading the question.

Willie was quick to offer his six-year-old bluntness. "Oh, she's in the barn milking, but I don't think she wants to see you."

Daniel wanted to nudge him to be quiet but there was no time.

"Oh, I'm sure she could use some help with the milking," Jasper said gesturing toward the barn. "You'll just have to remind me, how many udders do cows have?"

"Actually, we milk goats," Daniel said trying to suppress a smile, "and they have one udder with two teats."

"Oh, yeah, of course." Jasper started walking toward the barn. "Come on, Willie. Are you going to show me where we do the milking?"

The two young ladies spying through the barn door exchanged a look of panic. "He's coming in here! What do we do?" Hannah asked.

"I don't know. How badly do you want to avoid him? We could climb up into the hayloft quick!"

"I don't really feel like talking to him, but if he's coming in here I guess we can give him a good dose of farm reality. I don't think he'll like it." Hannah smirked.

"You're terrible!" Grace said slapping her friend's arm playfully.

The door opened and Daniel, Willie and Jasper stepped into the milk house. The next few minutes were both awkward and humorous, as Jasper tried and failed miserably to impress Hannah with his milking skills. It was all he could handle when the goat he was trying to milk kicked over the bucket, and spilled milk all over his nice pants.

"You've got to be kidding me!" he said, standing up and attempting to brush the milk off of himself. He looked utterly disgusted. "Why don't you train your goats not to stomp? I knew farming wasn't for me! Guys, I wish I could stay for supper, but I have to go home and change out of these pants."

The boys escorted him back to his truck, and, though they felt slightly bad about his pants getting covered in milk, they were glad to see him leave. Daniel went back into the house and Willie returned to the barn.

"I guess he didn't get the message last time that I wasn't interested in him." Hannah chuckled.

"He's pretty persistent," Grace said, resuming her milking job.

"Yeah," Willie said casually, "I told Mark about when he came and gave Dad a ride in his truck!"

"You did what? When did you talk to Mark?" Hannah was surprised.

Pressing Toward the Mark

"A long time ago. Grace's phone was ringing so I answered it and talked to Mark."

"What did you tell him about Jasper?" A slight tone of concern came through in Hannah's voice.

"I told him that Jasper wants to marry you, and came to our house, and Dad talked to him for a long time . . . and after that he and Dad went for a drive in his big truck."

"But did you tell him that there's no way in the world I would marry Jasper?!"

Willie just shrugged his shoulders. He observed his sister's concern that Mark may have gotten the wrong message. "It's okay. I can call Mark and tell him that you only want to marry him and not Jasper."

"No, don't do that, Willie," Grace said coming to Hannah's aid. "Next time, just give me the phone when my brother calls."

"Okay."

"Thanks, Buddy," Hannah said smoothing things over.

Willie left to finish his chores and the two ladies kept talking.

"Grace, have you heard how Mark's doing? Charlie told my parents more about Mark's experiences in Colombia. Do you think his heart has changed?"

Grace knew undoubtedly that Hannah still loved Mark deeply. "Well, over the summer I didn't have a chance to talk to him much . . . but we've talked a lot on the phone since he got back from Colombia. I think God has definitely been growing him a lot in many ways, especially through the kidnapping experience. But I don't want you to get your hopes up. You need to give him time to prove that his love for the Lord is greater than his love for anything or anyone else."

"I know. I'm trying not to get my hopes up. I told the Lord I am not going to push for Mark and me to get back together. I'm praying that if God wants it to happen, He will lead Mark to make the first move."

Chapter Fourteen

*I*t was the third week of September. Grace and Zack traveled to Alabama to visit her parents, as well as Mark, Charlie, Sarah, and the baby. Zack didn't get to see his sister Sarah much since she and Charlie had moved, so this was a good opportunity. Grace was eager to see her brother again, and observe first hand if his heart had changed. She wasn't too sure it had, but Hannah always seemed so hopeful. "Don't forget," Hannah would remind her, "God does amazing things."

During their week-long visit, Grace was blessed to find the old Mark . . . the brother who initiated spiritual conversations . . . the young man who diligently memorized Scripture and shared it with others . . . the one who spoke truth into every situation, and longed for souls to be saved. This was the brother she missed . . . and the man Hannah loved.

There was one thing she wanted to clear up before going home.

"Mark," she started randomly one evening as she sat watching him and her husband play a game of chess. Mark was leaning forward analyzing his next move. "Do you remember Willie telling you about a guy named Jasper?"

Mark sat up slowly taking a deep breath. "How could I forget," he said a little dryly.

"Well, I think Willie unintentionally gave you the wrong idea. Hannah is not interested in Jasper and never was."

Mark let out the deep breath he had been holding since the moment she mentioned that name. "What?" he said, not sure if he heard her right.

"Yeah. The guy was totally not suited for her. His fancy big truck didn't impress her . . . and neither did his milking skills . . . or anything else about him for that matter!" Grace said with a laugh.

"You mean she . . . I mean . . . is she seeing anyone else?"

"Nope," Grace said, glancing at Zack with a twinkle in her eye. She knew exactly where Hannah's heart was at, but she wondered if it was her place to share that with Mark?

"All this time, I thought . . . well from what Willie said, it sounded like this Jasper guy had stepped in and taken my place." He felt a little humiliated to say this, but it was true.

"That's not what happened at all. Mark, I'm not promising that things will ever be the same as they used to be . . . but I think it would be good for you to show your face in Indiana again."

Zack nodded in agreement.

"What does that mean?" Mark questioned.

"You left after a painful break-up. You aren't the only one who was hurt. Hannah was heart broken, and her family grieved losing you as a future brother and son."

Mark nodded thoughtfully. "I know, and I'm really sorry about that. But do you think going back would help things?"

"It could. If nothing else, just talk to them and let them know you have no hard feelings, and that you appreciate what they have invested into you over the years."

"I'll think about it. Sounds like it could be really awkward . . . but I want to do what's right."

Grace smiled, as she envisioned Hannah's prayers being answered.

"If I do go, it won't be right away though," Mark added after thinking for a minute. "On Friday I'm heading back to Colorado for a week. Elu Wanbli, from the hotel I lived at for a while, asked me to help lead a boys' wilderness camping trip out there."

"Sounds like a good opportunity! I want to hear all about it afterwards," Grace encouraged. Then she added with a hint of playfulness in her voice, "Just another reason for you to make your way back to Indiana!"

Upon their return home Grace and Zack had a conversation with Mr. and Mrs. Kallenbach about their

Pressing Toward the Mark

observations. They reported the same good news that Charlie had been telling them. Mark was on the right path again.

Once again, Denver, Colorado welcomed Mark Evans to his temporary home. Elu Wanbli was eager to have his help with the boys' wilderness camping trip.

The entire Wanbli family greeted Mark with smiles and hugs. Before the young campers were dropped off at the hotel, Elu sat down with Mark to explain his plans. They would take a 15-passenger van full of boys into the mountains and camp, hike, study the Bible, and have important conversations about practical, real life situations. Elu loved to use nature to teach about the Creator. His Native American ancestors worshipped the creation, more than the Creator. But he was overjoyed to personally know and worship only the Creator, who made all things.

At noon, the dining room at Dinever buzzed with twelve extra youngsters, between the ages of eight and twelve. Elu announced that this would be the last home-cooked meal for a while. The rest of the week they would be preparing their own food, some of which they would have to find along the trail.

A murmur of hushed voices arose.

"Don't worry," he assured them. "We won't let you starve. We are going to have a great time . . . BUT you'll need to be tough! This trip is not for quitters. There will be times when we feel like quitting . . . turning back . . . going home...but we can't listen to those feelings. Instead, we're going to practice asking God to help us complete challenges with courage! Are you ready, Boys???"

"Yeah!" they cheered, catching Elu's enthusiasm.

"Then eat up, and we'll leave here in about thirty minutes!"

The first day was fairly easy. The boys were fresh and energetic. From the place where they parked the van, the crew carried their backpacks and other supplies down a narrow path for about a mile. When they reached the spot where they would set up camp, Mark directed the boys on what to do. There was plenty to do . . . but . . . not every boy wanted to work. Particularly one nine-year-old, Jacob, made that clear. He sat aside by himself, absorbed in his cell phone. Elu noticed him first.

"Hey, Mark, can you keep the momentum going? I need to have a talk with Jacob."

Mark nodded, and Elu trotted over to the place where the boy was sitting. Around ten minutes later, he came back and informed Mark with an exasperated look on his face, that the boy was *not* easy to work with. "I took his phone," he said, patting the pocket it was in. "He knew before we left that we have a 'no phones' rule for all the boys on this trip."

"Do you think he's a trouble maker?" Mark asked doubtfully.

"No, not really. Just a hurting kid who tries to crawl into his own little world, instead of facing reality." He turned in the boy's direction, glad to see him helping some older boys set up a tent. "We'll just have to keep an eye on him."

By day four, it was clear to Elu that Jacob thought the world of Mark. If Elu wanted to get something across to the boy, he might as well send Mark. Anything "Mr. Mark" said was the best idea ever! The rest of the boys looked up to Mark, but Elu had successfully gained their respect too.

The wilderness trip was a stretching experience for everyone . . . leaders included. They would set up camp, and then explore, and hike in the mountains all day, returning at sunset for another night at that campsite. The next day, they hiked further and set up camp in a new spot. Then the pattern repeated. Each day was infused with Biblical character-building lessons. Either Mark or Elu would teach on the trail as they went, using their natural surroundings as illustrations. Each morning began with personal time with God for every camper. Then was calisthenics time, when Elu would lead them in push-ups, burpees, crunches, and more. In the evening, they would sit around a fire, sing, tell stories, and do a devotional together. Then everyone would lay down on the grass and look at the starry sky. For ten straight minutes, no one was to talk, but only pray silently to God, and think about what they had learned that day. Mark enjoyed this quiet time each night. On their last night in the mountains, Mark reflected on all that had taken place that week. *So many boys in this day and age are starving for godly male role models. Jacob is a prime example of that. I'm probably the first man who has cared enough to sit and talk with him ever! Our society isn't helping anything, teaching boys to become girly, wimpy cowards.* Mark prayed about ways he could encourage other men to lead by example and reach out to boys for God's glory.

The wilderness camping trip ended Saturday afternoon back at the hotel. Parents came to pick up their worn out but happy boys, and good-byes were exchanged. Mark talked with Jacob and his parents, and they were honored by his request to stay in contact.

The following morning, Mark joined the Wanbli's at their church. An African American woman in her forties shared a testimony during the service. She smiled nervously as she scanned the crowd of faces looking back at her.

"Hello everyone. My name is Marsha," she began in a deep southern accent. "The Pastor asked me to share this story with you. He thought it would encourage y'all. A couple months ago, I had an opportunity to share the gospel when I was at work. Yes, I know – I could get in trouble for this. But when someone's soul is hangin' in the balance, Brothers and Sisters, we better speak up!"

A few amens echoed across the sanctuary.

"I work as a paramedic. This one day, as the ambulance was makin' its way back to the Newport Central Hospital, somethin' in me said this kid lyin' on the stretcher was not gunna pull through. He was conscious, but he had taken a bad fall in a rock climbing accident."

Mark's expression changed. He sat up straight and listened intently.

"I axed him if he knew Jesus. He said he had seen pictures of Jesus hanging on a cross, but he didn't know why. Can you believe it, Brothers and Sisters? A young man who grew up all his life in America . . . knew that a man called Jesus died on the cross . . . but no one took the time to explain to him why!

"As the ambulance continued toward the hospital, I glanced up at my two EMT coworkers, knowin' they might get me in trouble for 'proselytizing' a patient. It didn't matter. I told that young man on the stretcher the reason Jesus died...and that he rose again victorious over sin and death. Hallelujah, he heard the gospel and believed right there on the ambulance!"

The congregation began to clap and a few shouts of "Hallelujah!" and "Praise the Lord!" rang out.

Then Marsha concluded her story. "After we moved him off of the ambulance I never saw him again. I don't have any idea what happened to him after that. But what I do know is he's either bound for glory, or he's in glory right now, praisin' the Lord for savin' him! I am so thankful God allowed me to talk with him that day! Is there someone that God would have you share with today?"

With that, she stepped off of the platform and took her seat. Mark's mind felt stunned, as if it had been shocked with a whopping surge of electricity. Had it been Jerome on that ambulance? He had to talk to this lady.

As soon as the service was over, he intentionally made his way over to her and introduced himself.

"I had a friend who had a fatal rock climbing accident the beginning of August," Mark explained. "He was taken to Newport Central Hospital."

Marsha tilted her head and raised one eyebrow.

"Do you remember the name of the guy on the ambulance?" Mark hoped she would.

"Hmm . . . ." She thought for a moment. "I really have no idea. I can describe him for you though. He was fairly short . . . had sandy blond hair . . ."

"Was he wearing anything on his head when you found him?"

"Oh, yes! How could I forget? He was wearing a bright tie-dyed bandanda around his forehead."

"I'm sure it was Jerome then! He always wore that bandana."

"Jerome! Yes, that was his name! I remember now that you say it. He must have had a great sense of humor because he cracked a joke even when we all knew he was in a bad state." She continued talking, but to Mark it was as if her voice trailed off into the background.

He swallowed hard trying suppress a sudden wave of emotion as he realized the implications of Marsha's story. He had not done his part in sharing the gospel with Jerome. But God had a servant on the ambulance that day who was willing to speak up. He had given Jerome one last chance to be saved before he went into a coma and never woke up again. "Thank you so much," Mark said softly, emphasizing every word. His friend was in heaven after all.

Pressing Toward the Mark

Mark's phone beeped as he got back into his car after refueling. He picked it up from the passenger seat to look at the text that had come in. It was from Jessa. He hadn't heard much from her since the day he had visited her in the hospital.

Hi Mark, I just want to say thanks again for allowing God to use you in my life to bring me to the Lord.

Mark typed a quick reply. *You're welcome. Praise the Lord!*

The phone beeped again. *I am back in California with my family, and God is giving me joy and contentment. We've had some tough things to work through, but God is gracious and I am seeing Him bless us as we seek to do His will.*

Great to hear, Mark texted back. *God is good. I have some super awesome news I thought you'd want to know. I just found out that Jerome got saved before he died!!! Call me when you get a chance and I'll tell you about it.* Mark hit the send button, set it back down on the passenger seat and then started his car.

As the miles passed he mused upon the truth of what Jessa said. *God is gracious. God blesses those who seek Him. God gives joy and contentment.* Those truths were the one medicine that would counteract the burning in his stomach, and the tense nerves across his entire body. A silent battle raged in his heart and mind. What if Mr. and Mrs. Kallenbach would totally misunderstand his reason for coming. What if they thought he was just trying to win Hannah back? What if they thought his decision to minister in the U.S. was just a loser's way of sounding like he was willing to be a missionary when he really wasn't? Especially after hearing about his capture by the guerrillas, they would probably think he was just afraid of something like that happening again.

Mark pressed the knob on the radio to listen to the CD he had inserted earlier. He was developing the habit of listening to the audio Bible while on the road. The CD started playing at Philippians chapter three. As the very familiar passage was read, certain verses stood out and seemed so applicable for him today.

Brethren, I count not myself to have apprehended: but this one thing I do, forgetting those things which are behind, and reaching forth unto those things which are before,

I press toward the mark for the prize of the high calling of God in Christ Jesus.

Be careful for nothing; but in every thing by prayer and supplication with thanksgiving let your requests be made known unto God.

And the peace of God, which passeth all understanding, shall keep your hearts and minds through Christ Jesus.

Finally, brethren, whatsoever things are true, whatsoever things are honest, whatsoever things are just, whatsoever things are pure, whatsoever things are lovely, whatsoever things are of good report; if there be any virtue, and if there be any praise, think on these things.

I can do all things through Christ which strengtheneth me.

Pressing Toward the Mark

(Philippians 3:13-14, 4:6-8, 4:13)

When the book of Philippians concluded, Mark turned off the CD for a few minutes. "Lord, I choose to trust You with this whole situation. It's in Your hands. You know my heart...You know my motives...and I'm doing this for You, not for myself or even the Kallenbachs. Let Your will be done, and Your Name be glorified as I tell them what You have been doing in my life."

It wasn't until late that night that Mark arrived "home" in Indiana. He found his little house the same as he had left it, but if felt so cold and empty without his sister Grace living there as before. After a short night's sleep, he took a quick shower, shaved, and read in his Bible for a while. He had texted Mr. Kallenbach the day before and arranged to meet with him and his wife at 9:00 a.m.

As Mark turned in at the Kallenbach farm, two boys on dusty four-wheelers met him at the end of the driveway. Daniel and Joey had been excitedly waiting for him to arrive so they could "escort" him to the house. Once Mark had parked the car and stepped out onto the driveway, the two boys gave him a hearty welcome.

Tyler came flying out of the side door of the house to join the welcome committee.

"We are so glad you're back!" Joey started.

"Yeah, we've really missed you!" Tyler added. "Mom and Dad are waiting for you inside. I guess we aren't allowed to be part of your meeting." His face spoke to the fact that he felt it was an unnecessary injustice to be excluded from such an important conversation.

Pressing Toward the Mark

"Come one, Guys," Daniel suggested, "let's let him talk with Mom and Dad, and they'll tell us what we need to know."

"Thanks, Guys," Mark said in a humble tone. "I missed you a lot too."

Hannah's parents met him at the door and greeted him warmly like old times. It was strange being back in this very familiar home, with these people who had virtually become family. The last time he had sat across from Mr. Kallenbach and talked was the day of Grace's wedding.... He couldn't let his mind wander back to that though. *Forgetting those things which are behind, and reaching forth unto those things which are before,* he reminded himself, *I press toward the mark....*

Chapter Fifteen

"Grace, I am so excited and nervous, I don't know what to do with myself!" Hannah's voice almost sang over the phone.

Grace smiled. "I'm excited for you, Hannah!"

"As you know," Hannah continued, "I have been praying so much for Mark over the summer...and now God is bringing him back! Mom and Dad were so thrilled by the change they saw in him when they talked earlier this week."

"That's great!"

"Yes. And, Grace, remember when you said that Mark needed to prove that his love for the Lord was greater than his love for anything or anyone else?"

"Yeah."

"Well, I think he has. He told Dad about his plans for ministry in the States, knowing that my dream has been *foreign* missions. Dad said Mark didn't think I would marry him if he wasn't a foreign missionary. His decision shows that he's willing to follow God's lead, no matter what the cost."

"I agree, Hannah. And I'm really glad. So you and your parents are meeting with Mark tonight?"

"Yeah, at 7:00. My parents and I have talked and prayed a lot these past few days, and I am ready to start the courtship again if Mark thinks it's God's will. We're going to discuss that tonight."

Grace closed her eyes for a second and smiled, "I know my brother, Hannah. And I know he still loves you. He's been praying about this and leaving it in God's hands. If you are willing to resume the relationship, I'm 99% sure he is too."

"I'll let you know how it goes tonight," Hannah said wrapping up the conversation.

"Thanks. I'll be praying for you guys!"

"Thank you, Grace. I am so blessed to have a best friend like you."

"Ditto, Hannah. I'll talk to you tomorrow."

"Sounds good, bye!" Hannah set the phone down on the table next to her. She stood up quickly, determining to take a brisk walk. Maybe that would help her to calm down and be ready in her mind for tonight.

Pressing Toward the Mark

It was now the first week of October. Mark and Hannah resumed their courtship with the blessing of their parents. The Kallenbach children were very happy to have their "big brother" back . . . although they didn't like how he sometimes forgot about them and only thought about Hannah. Joey tried to explain it to his younger brothers. "It's a plague called La-la-land, and it happens to all people who are in love. Remember, Charlie came down with it when he fell in love with Sarah. The thing about this plague is that the person with the disease doesn't recognize any of the symptoms. Guys, we just have to bear with them and be patient. Let's just be thankful we have Mark at all!"

Hannah and Mark discussed in depth their intentions and desires for ministry. Though Hannah had envisioned herself on the foreign mission field, God had also shown her a need for missionaries in her own country. If God was leading the man she loved to serve stateside, she could joyfully support him in that. As plans developed, Mr. Kallenbach asked Mark if he would be interested in staying in Indiana and helping build their small and dying home church. This was a big task and not quite as exciting as some opportunities. However, this little fellowship of believers had been meeting for several years with no real growth or direction. They needed fresh energy, clear goals, and realistic objectives. They needed someone who could dedicate time and attention to building the church. Mark also recognized the need for true men of God to visit patients in the local hospital – a ministry which the town had been lacking for years.

It was true: there were plenty of other options for ministry, but Hannah and Mark both felt this was where God wanted them right now. They knew some day God might lead them elsewhere . . . perhaps even to a foreign field. And if so, they were both willing to go.

As November rolled in, Mark decided it was time to sit down with Hannah's father and ask the same question he had asked that day of Grace's wedding: Would he give his permission and blessing for Hannah and him to marry? This time, though, so much was different. Mark felt the new strength of character that God had built in him, and he trusted that God's will would be done. Mr. Kallenbach readily gave his blessing, his wife also being in agreement.

Plans for a February wedding were soon underway. Mark made the needed adjustments to his house to accommodate a wife. Grace gave him some helpful tips, as this type of thing was not his forte.

New local ministry opportunities seemed to surface with each passing week. When Mark resumed his job as a plumber part-time, he discovered how much even this was an opportunity to minister and witness to those in the workplace.

Mark initiated meetings with the men of their small church to develop a purpose statement and make plans for going forward. His dedication and excitement kindled fresh enthusiasm among the others. This little congregation was heading in a positive direction at last.

The wedding day was a beautiful one. A fresh layer of light reflective snow covered the little town, making it look like a perfect painting. To Mark and Hannah, that day *was* like a perfect painting... a bright and beautiful dream that scarcely seemed real. The day had started early with so many things to do before guests arrived. Then, it seemed, the next moment the sanctuary was flooded with supportive friends and family. The ceremony Mark and Hannah had so thought and prayed over had finally come, and it was time to pledge their devotion and commitment to each other. Mark watched as his lovely bride gracefully walked down the aisle to be his wife. *Lord, I don't deserve this precious gift. Thank you!* He prayed silently as his eyes welled up with tears.

The fresh snow made for gorgeous pictures. The photographer instructed the bride and groom to pose for one last picture before going back to the church for the reception.

"Okay, hold it right there... perfect," Click, click, click. "Alright, fantastic!" she said folding up her tripod. "You're set to go. You can go in and warm up now!"

Mark grabbed Hannah's hand gently, as the photographer headed back to the building. He seemed to be saying, "Let's wait... there's one more thing." She was wondering if he was thinking the same thing she was.

"Let's thank God together before we go back."

Hannah smiled. That was exactly what she wanted to do.

The new husband and wife knelt down in the snow, and praised the One who had brought them together.

"Lord God, You are so good. We just want to thank You and praise You for loving us and saving us...thank You for walking with us through life in the good times and the bad.

Pressing Toward the Mark

Thank You for Your forgiveness, and for being patient with us. We love You more than anything else, Lord. We chose to put You first...before each other and before all others." Mark paused for a moment, taking a long deep breath. "Thank You for showing me what really matters in life: living for You and bringing souls to Christ . . . no matter where or who they are. Take us, Lord, and use us in any way You choose. We pray this all in the name of our precious Savior, Jesus. Amen."

Mark stood up and offered his hand to his new wife. "Come on, we better not keep our guests waiting any longer."

And with that, they walked back hand in hand, excited to be used of the Lord, and to "press toward the mark". . . together.

The End

About the Author

Karen was born abroad in the Marshall Islands and to this day loves tropics and travel. Her thirst for adventure drives her to try new things often, and provides her with interesting experiences to write about. She loves to teach important life lessons and spiritual principles through fiction. Karen lives with her parents and five siblings on their busy farmstead in the beautiful hills of Mondovi, Wisconsin. She is blessed to be a part of the family's outreach, Together for Truth Ministries.

Some of her many interests include: teaching English as a second language, camping and backpacking, learning foreign languages, mission work, and ministry to Spanish-speaking people. She is passionate about memorizing Scripture and sharing the gospel of salvation.

For more information or to order additional copies of

Pressing Toward the Mark,

please contact us:

Mailing address:

P.O. Box 331

Eleva, WI 54738

Email:

1peter5511@gmail.com

Website:

www.BooksByKarenForster.blogspot.com